Knights of Pythias

First Digest of the Laws of the Supreme Lodge of the World

Knights of Pythias

Knights of Pythias

First Digest of the Laws of the Supreme Lodge of the World
Knights of Pythias

ISBN/EAN: 9783337286828

Printed in Europe, USA, Canada, Australia, Japan

Cover: Foto ©Andreas Hilbeck / pixelio.de

More available books at **www.hansebooks.com**

FIRST

DIGEST OF THE LAWS

OF

THE SUPREME LODGE

OF THE WORLD,

LEONARD, PU

105-107-109 MADISON STREET

1877.

INTRODUCTORY.

In the compilation of this work the publishers have endeavored to make it at once exhaustive, correct, and easy of reference.

The subjects are presented alphabetically, and in order to prevent repetitions are placed under the *most appropriate* head, with cross references where necessary. For instance, under the head of " Membership " are many subjects which might be looked for under the head of " Subordinate Lodges"; these, under the latter caption, have cross references to " Charters and Dispensations, Constitution, Membership," etc.

In many instances explanatory notes will be found. These are simply an expression of the views of the compiler, based upon a careful examination of the subject, and have no bearing except so far as they recommend themselves to the reader.

In the preparation of the work the publishers are under many obligations for the assistance and encouragement extended by several distinguished members of the Order: more especially to SAMUEL J. WILLETT, *Grand Chancellor of Illinois*, and his associate officers, S. J. FREEMAN and J. D. ROPER; also to D. A. CASHMAN, *Supreme Representative for Illinois and Chairman of the Committee on Unwritten Work of the Supreme Lodge*, who by request, conjointly with T. W. DEERING, M.D., *Past Supreme Representative for Kansas*, made a critical examination of the work previous to its going to press.

CHICAGO, *May 1, 1877.*

DIGEST OF LAWS.

ACROATIC AGENDA.
[See Ritual.]

AGE.
[See Membership.]

AMENDMENTS.
[See Constitution.]

ANNIVERSARY OF THE ORDER.
[See Pythian Period.]

1. **The 19th day of February** is declared to be and established as the anniversary of the organization of the Order. (*Jour. 1875, 1149.*)

APPEALS AND WRITS OF ERROR.

1. Constitutional provisions.
2. What is an appeal.
3. Consent thereto.
4. Appellant must show interest.
5. To what tribunal.
6. Appeal papers: (a) *How authenticated;* (b) *contents;* (c) *to whom sent;* (d) *lost.*
7. Appeal, how to be heard in Grand Lodge.

[See, also, Supreme Lodge ; Committees.]

(1) CONSTITUTIONAL PROVISIONS.

2. **All appeals and writs of error** taken from the action or decision of a Grand Lodge, or a Subordinate Lodge under the immediate jurisdiction of the Supreme

Lodge of the World, to said Supreme Lodge, as hereinafter provided, shall be received and passed upon by said Supreme Lodge, in its capacity as a court of last resort; but in all cases the action or decision of a Grand Lodge, or a Subordinate Lodge under the immediate jurisdiction of the Supreme Lodge, shall be final and conclusive until reversed by this Supreme Lodge, on appeals or prosecutions of a writ of error therefrom, as hereinafter provided. (*Const., Art. xix, Sec. 1.*)

Query, Would this be construed *literally* when the question involved payment of monies where the same could not be recovered if once expended,—for instance, an unconstitutional assessment; also, in the case of infliction of punishment, which if inflicted could not be undone,—such as reprimand? Would not an appeal, in either case, justly act as a *supersedeas?*

3. An appeal may be taken from the action or decision of any Subordinate Lodge under the immediate jurisdiction of the Supreme Lodge of the World, to said Supreme Lodge, by any member of such Subordinate Lodge, or by any other person whose rights have been denied by such action or decision, upon giving written notice to said Subordinate Lodge of said appeal within two weeks from and after such action or decision. (*Const., Art. xix, Sec. 2.*)

4. With the consent of a Grand Lodge, an appeal may be taken by any Subordinate Lodge, or member under its jurisdiction, from any action or decision of such Grand Lodge, to the Supreme Lodge of the World; provided, however, that such consent shall not be necessary when a suspended or dissolved Lodge, after having surrendered to its Grand Lodge all its effects, books and property, appeals from such decision; and, provided, further, that any action or decision of a Grand Lodge, where is drawn in question any provision of the Constitution, or any enactment or authority of the Supreme Lodge of the World, and the action or decision is against the validity of such provision, enactment or authority, may be examined and reversed or affirmed in the Supreme Lodge of the World, upon a writ of error, to the same extent as could have been done upon an appeal legally taken from such action or decision. (*Const., Art. xix, Sec. 3.*)

5. Such writ of error, as provided for by the last section, may be issued by and upon petition to either the

Grand Chancellor of the Grand Lodge, the action or decision of which is sought to be reviewed, the Supreme Chancellor or the Supreme Lodge of the World, in the case provided for in the last section, and in the order only as above
named in this section. (*Const., Art. xix, Sec. 4.*)

6. **Consent** of a Grand Lodge to appeal must be obtained
at the same session at which the action or decision, from
which such appeal is sought to be taken, was had, and the
proper record upon such appeal must be transmitted, properly
attested, to the next session of the Supreme Lodge thereafter; provided, that the Supreme Lodge may, in extreme
cases, allow the appeal to be entertained at not later than
its next following session thereafter. The same rules shall
also apply in the prosecution of a writ of error. (*Const.,
Art. xix, Sec. 5.*)

7. The Supreme Lodge of the World may also adopt
such additional rules and regulations as may be deemed
necessary and proper to fully carry into effect the foregoing
provisions of this article. (*Const., Art. xix, Sec. 6.*)

(2) WHAT IS AN APPEAL.

8. A simple statement of the facts of a case is not an
appeal. (*Jour. 1870, 204.*)

(3) CONSENT THERETO.

9. It is the duty of all Grand Lodges to permit appeals to come up, and they must furnish all testimony and
papers required, properly attested. (*Jour. 1871, 404.*)

10. In the case of the appeal of J. P. M. against the
action of the Grand Lodge of California, where consent
that the appeal be taken was given by the Grand Chancellor, the appeal was dismissed, it not having received the
consent of the Grand Lodge of California to be brought
before the Supreme Lodge. (*Jour. 1873, 732.*)

[See Constitutional provisions on the subject, *ante.*]

(4) APPELLANT MUST SHOW INTEREST.

11. Where A. C. D., a Supreme Representative, failed to
attend a session of the Supreme Lodge, and the committee
appointed by the Grand Lodge to investigate the cause
reported in favor of vacating his seat, which report was

adopted by the Grand Lodge, from which action an appeal was taken to the Supreme Lodge by two Past Chancellors, on the ground that the Supreme Representative, whose seat was vacated, had not had a fair trial in accordance with their Constitution; it was *ruled*, that, although *all* brothers are *entitled to*, and should be given, a *fair* trial, yet, without entering fully into the merits of the case, the only aggrieved party in the case was Rep. A. C. D.; and as he had failed to appeal to the Supreme Lodge, the appellants had not the right of appeal, they not being directly interested in the matter, and the appeal was dismissed. (*Jour. 1875, 1122.*)

(5) To what Tribunal.

12. The subject-matter appealed must first be acted upon by the Grand Lodge, before an appeal can be taken by a Subordinate Lodge to the Supreme Lodge. (*Jour. 1874, 939.*)

13. An appeal does not lie directly from the decision of the Grand Chancellor of a State to the Supreme Lodge; but the proper practice in such case is to appeal from the decision of the Grand Chancellor to the Grand Lodge, and from the decision of that body an appeal lies to the Supreme Lodge. (*Jour. 1875, 1131.*)

This ruling, while in conformity with the law previous to 1874. and as it now stands, yet under the Constitution adopted in 1874, which was in force when this ruling was made, would seem to be erroneous. as, under Art. XIX of Constitution, page 960, Jour. 1874, "Appeals in proper form shall come up without any intervention or prevention of Grand or Subordinate Lodges, and where presented for certification by their official seal, the same shall be done."

(6) Appeal Papers: (*a*) How Authenticated.

14. Appeal papers from the decision of a Grand Lodge to the Supreme Lodge should be authenticated by the signatures of the Grand Chancellor and Grand Keeper of Records and Seal, with the seal of the Grand Lodge attached. (*Jour. 1871, 404; 1875, 1132.*)

(*b*) What they should Contain.

15. The papers on an appeal from the action of a Grand Lodge to the Supreme Lodge should contain a certified copy of the proceedings of the Grand Lodge complained of. (*Jour. 1876, 1309.*)

(c) To Whom Sent.

16. All appeals to the Supreme Lodge, and accompanying papers, must be sent to the Supreme R. and C. S. at least one month previous to the annual session of the Supreme Lodge. And the Supreme R. and C. S. shall at that time place all appeals and accompanying papers in the hands of the chairman of the Committee on Appeals, to enable said committee to carefully review the same; also the law bearing upon them, and report fully and promptly to the Supreme Lodge at its session.

No appeal will be entertained by the Supreme Lodge if not in compliance with the above requirement, except by vote of the Supreme Lodge. (*Jour. 1872, 563.*)

This was enacted prior to the new Constitution, but seems to be applicable now with the substitution of Supreme K. of R. and S. in place of the Supreme R. and C. S.

(d) Papers Lost.

17. Where an appeal case was recommitted at a previous session, and the papers were lost or mislaid, it was referred back to the Grand Lodge, from whose action it was taken, for a new trial. (*Jour. 1874, 939.*)

(7) How Heard in Grand Lodge.

18. An appeal from the decision of the Committee of Appeals of a Grand Lodge should be heard by the Grand Lodge; and it is improper to refer the action of such committee to a special committee for investigation. (*Jour. 1870, 178; 1871, 400.*)

APPOINTMENT.
[See Election and Appointment.]

ARREARS.
[See Dues; Benefits.]

ASSESSMENTS.
[See Insurance; Revenue.]

BALLOT.

[See, also, Membership ; Offenses ; Supreme Lodge.]

(1) Constitutional Provisions; Black Balls.

19. Grand Lodges may legislate in their local law to prescribe that one black ball may reject, in cases of application for membership, but shall not increase the same to more than as prescribed in the Supreme maximum of *two.* (*Const., Art. xxv.*)

20. Applicants for initiation shall be balloted for by secret ball ballot, and if approved may be admitted. (*Const., Art. viii, Sec. 2.*)

21. Should two black balls appear against a candidate, the ballot shall be renewed immediately. Should two or more appear on the second ballot, he shall be declared rejected, and no other ballot shall be taken in his case for the space of six months thereafter. [Obligatory.] (*Const., Art. viii, Sec. 2; old Const., Sec. 3, Art. v, Sub. Lodge.*)

22. In balloting, two (2) black balls appearing, a second ballot is ordered *at once;* two (2) or more appearing on the second ballot, he is rejected. Should three (3) black balls appear on the first ballot, it requires no other ballot to be taken at all. (*Jour. 1873, App. 38.*)

[See a contrary decision by D. G. C. of Ala. in Jour. 1872, 476.]

(2) Inspected by Whom.

23. A ballot for a candidate for membership should be inspected by the Vice Chancellor, and the result announced by the Chancellor Commander. (*Jour. 1876, 1227, 1296.*)

(3) On Application by Card.

24. The old Constitution being repealed, the present law requires the same ballot on an application by card as for an application for membership by initiation. (*Jour. 1875, 1042, 1114; Const., Art. viii, Sec. 2.*)

(4) On Application for Advancement.

25. If a Page is rejected on a ballot for the rank of Esquire, or an Esquire is rejected on a ballot for the rank of Knight, another ballot may be had in either case in one month thereafter. The new Constitution makes no distinction between this case and balloting on an application for initiation as a Page, which is regarded as an omission rather than intent: *Provided*, that this decision shall only apply to Lodges under the immediate jurisdiction of the Supreme Lodge. (*Jour. 1875, 1043, 1114.*)

(5) By Applicants for a Dispensation.

26. The dropping of a name from the list of applicants for a dispensation by a ballot by all the applicants, while it virtually has the effect, among those who are interested at the time, of a rejection of the name so dropped, yet does not estop the party whose name has been "dropped" from applying in a regular way, and taking the chances of a legal ballot when or after the Lodge is legally instituted; neither does the "dropping" of the name in the first instance constitute him a black-balled or rejected party, or prevent him from applying to that or any other Lodge of the Order in a regular way, and under the local laws of jurisdiction or territory where residing. (*Jour. 1873, App. 40.*)

BANNER.

27. At the session of the Supreme Lodge, of 1873, a banner for the Order was adopted, as follows:

To be composed of three pieces of silk, of color and sizes as follows: *Dark Blue*, size 18 by 30 inches; *Orange-Yellow*, size 18 by 30; *Crimson*, size 24 by 36. Colors to be placed as per accompanying diagram. The full size of banner to be 3 by 4½ feet. Shield in center *painted in white*, size 18 by 24 inches. The device on shield to be the distinction of rank of Lodge—*Supreme, Grand,* or *Subordinate.*

For Supreme Lodge.—A Globe, and in circle around it to be the words, "Supreme Lodge of the World, Knights of Pythias."

For Grand Lodges.— Grand Lodge or State Seal, and in

circle around same, "Grand Lodge of ——, Knights of Pythias."

For Subordinate Lodges.—K. P. Cut as on accompanying diagram, with name and number of Lodge, together with location (viz., "Excelsior Lodge, No. 9, K. of P., Cincinnati, Ohio"); on edge of banner, all around, fine gold lines one and one-half inches wide; on bottom, gilt fringe three or three and one-half inches deep. Staff to be of oak or other suitable wood seven or eight feet long; on top of staff, spear-head; ball and falcon spear-heads on end of cross-piece. All marks, devices, designs, etc., on banner to be in gold or gold and black. (*Jour. 1873, 687, 740.*)

It would seem that the Supreme Lodge, by the preambles of the resolution by which the above-described banner was adopted, repealed the prior legislation respecting a flag. The preambles and resolution in question are as follows:

"WHEREAS, A banner is more in conformity with the character of an idea associated with the Order of Knights of Pythias than the flag adopted by the Supreme Lodge; and,

"WHEREAS, Said flag is not in favor with or been adopted by the Subordinate Lodges in this jurisdiction;

"*Resolved*, That our representatives to the Supreme Lodge be instructed to use their influence toward the adoption by said Supreme Lodge of a banner for the Order, and we most cordially indorse and recommend the design presented by Bro. Chas. A. Bird, of Excelsior Lodge, No. 9, Cincinnati, Ohio."

BOARD OF TRUSTEES.

[See Incorporation.]

28. A "board of trustees" has no right to transcend its instructions and expend money without authority; and if it does, the Lodge will not be liable therefor. (*Jour. 1871, 374, 395.*)

BENEFITS; RELIEF FUNDS; DONATIONS.

1. Constitutional provisions.
2. Meaning and nature of benefits.
3. When to be paid.
4. How forfeited.
5. Funeral benefits.
6. Donations.
7. Fund for nursing sick brothers.

[See. also. Insurance; Committees; Dues.]

(1) CONSTITUTIONAL PROVISIONS.

29. Lodges shall provide for carrying into effect the beneficial character of the Order, by providing for the payment of weekly benefits in case of disability, and funeral benefits in case of the death of a member; and weekly benefits shall not be less than one dollar per week, nor funeral benefits less than twenty dollars. [Obligatory.] (*Const., Art. viii, Sec. 2.*)

[See note to clause 33, *infra.*]

(2) MEANING AND NATURE OF BENEFITS.

30. The term "benefits," as used in the [old] Subordinate Lodge Constitution, Art. ix, means all advantages and privileges. (*Jour. 1872, 585.*)

No reason is perceived why it does not mean the same under the new Constitution.

31. The claim of members of the Order to a certain fixed sum, designated by law, to be paid to them during sickness or inability to procure a livelihood during such sickness, is a right, and not a charity. (*Jour. 1873, 692, 753.*)

32. The payment of weekly and funeral benefits to sick members is a distinguishing characteristic of the Order, and may be regarded as a fundamental principle of the Order of Knights of Pythias. (*Jour. 1873, 693, 753.*)

33. It is the duty of all Subordinate Lodges to tax their members that they may be enabled to pay stipulated weekly and funeral benefits to sick members or the family, and that all Subordinate Lodges shall pay some weekly and funeral benefits. (*Jour. 1873, 693, 753.*)

This was under the old Constitution. The *minimum* amount is now prescribed by Constitution. (See *supra.*) The amount was formerly left to be fixed by the Subordinate Lodges. (*Jour. 1873, 692, 753.*) With the restrictions contained in the above-quoted constitutional provision the subject of benefits should be left to local jurisdictions. (*Jour. 1868, 18; 1872, 468, 613, 614.*)

(3) WHEN TO BE PAID.

34. It is competent for a Grand Lodge to prescribe any definite period of time within which Subordinate Lodges shall pay benefits. (*Jour. 1872, 588, 595.*)

(4) How Forfeited.
[See, also, Funeral Benefits.]

35. Fines and assessments cannot be added to dues, to work a forfeiture of membership or benefits, before the time specified in the laws of the Supreme, Grand, or Subordinate Lodges. (*Jour. 1876, 1228, 1284, 1296, 1300.*)

[See Dues.]

36. A brother who leaves the United States in impaired health, and who continues so after his departure, so that he is incapacitated from gaining a livelihood, is still entitled to benefits from his Lodge. (*Jour. 1875, 1148.*)

37. And the fact that after the brother's departure the following by-law was incorporated in the laws of the Subordinate Lodge — "A sick brother, while under the care of this Lodge, shall not leave the jurisdiction of the Relief Committee without forfeiting his weekly benefits, unless he shall have obtained the consent of the Relief Committee and the approval of the Lodge"—cannot affect his right to benefits. (*Jour. 1875, 1148.*)

38. J. R. O. was suspended from Mechanics Lodge, No. 33, of Maryland, for non-payment of dues, and was reinstated to membership on November 28, 1873, and on May 29, 1874, was reported to the Lodge as sick. On this night O. would owe the Lodge $2 (or one quarter's dues), and had been reinstated six months, and had been sick for nine days. He applied to his Lodge for benefits. The C. C. declared that O. was not entitled to benefits, because he had not been reinstated six months. From this decision O. appealed to the Grand Lodge, stating the Lodge had no by-laws fixing the time required to pass before a brother who had been reinstated becomes beneficial. This appeal was referred to the Committee on Appeals and Grievances (Grand Lodge). This committee decided that the brother had complied with all the laws, and was entitled to benefits, which action was sustained by the Grand Lodge. *Held*, on appeal to the Supreme Lodge, that the decision of the Grand Lodge was correct, and the appeal was dismissed. (*Jour. 1875, 1161.*)

39. The case of Mary L. G. *vs.* Lafayette Lodge, No. 25, of the Grand Jurisdiction of Maryland, is: Said M. L. G.

claims sick benefits for seventy-four weeks, or from May 10, 1871, to October 10, 1872. From the printed proceedings of the Grand Lodge of Maryland it appears that the aforesaid Lafayette Lodge, No. 25, was suspended nearly all the time mentioned above. Even on the day of the death of the brother (G.) the Lodge was not recognized by the Grand Lodge of Maryland. *Held*, that the deceased brother was not entitled to any benefits during such suspension; also, he being notified the Lodge was about being organized, and not paying any attention to the notification, he should not be considered a member of the aforesaid Lodge. The case was accordingly referred back to the Grand Lodge of Maryland to audit the accounts of the said Lafayette Lodge, No. 25, with directions that if any benefits were found due the said Bro. G. prior to the suspension of the aforesaid Lodge, and he entitled to them, -that the Grand Lodge order paid, without interest. (*Jour. 1874, 944.*)

(5) Funeral Benefits.

40. The question whether if a brother, while in good standing in his Subordinate Lodge, commits suicide, it does or not deprive his wife or nearest competent relative from receiving the funeral benefits of such brother, is entirely a matter of Grand Lodge legislation. (*Jour. 1873, 684, 734.*)

41. On appeal from the Grand Lodge of Maryland, the facts were as follows: G., who was in arrears $2 quarterly dues, and $1 funeral tax, applied to the Subordinate Lodge for benefits on account of the death of his wife, which application was denied, and this decision sustained by the Grand Lodge of that State. *Held*, that its decision was correct. (*Jour. 1876, 1307.*)

42. On appeal from the action of the Grand Lodge of the District of Columbia, relative to the action of a Subordinate Lodge in refusing to pay funeral benefits to the widow of G., where G. was reported, March 31, 1875, as having been sick since March 29, 1875, and on the same day G. caused to be paid to the Subordinate Lodge the sum of $3, he having been in arrears $2.74 at the time of his sickness: *Held*, affirming the decision of the Grand Lodge, that the widow was entitled to benefits. (*Jour. 1876, 1318.*)

43. In the matter of Laurel Lodge, No. 4, *vs.* The Grand Lodge, K. of P., of California, the facts were as follows:

The widow of A. W. (a deceased member of Laurel Lodge), applied for the sum of $60, being balance claimed to be due under a section of the By-Laws of said Lodge, which is as follows:

"Article XII, Sec. 2. On the death of a brother there shall be appropriated from the funds of the Lodge $100 to defray the funeral expenses."

Of that sum only $40 were expended by Laurel Lodge, $80 additional being contributed by other organizations. The Lodge deny the claim, on the ground that as the sum named in the By-Laws is not now needed for funeral expenses the Lodge is not bound to pay the balance of the $100. An appeal was taken by the widow to the Grand Lodge of California, which appeal was sustained. *Held*, that the decision of the Grand Lodge was correct, and that the widow was entitled to receive the sum of $60 from the funds of Laurel Lodge, No 4. (*Jour. 1872, 551, 589.*)

(6) DONATIONS.

44. A Subordinate Lodge can make a donation to a distressed brother in destitution and want within its own jurisdiction. (*Jour. 1876, 1308.*)

(7) FUND FOR NURSING SICK BROTHERS.

45. On appeal against the decision of the Grand Lodge of Kentucky, in 1875, the facts were as follows: Clay Lodge provides in its By-Laws a fund for nursing sick brothers. (See Sec. 6, Art. IV.) An order had been granted on the exchequer by a majority vote for this purpose. From the action of Clay Lodge L. appealed to the Grand Chancellor, on the ground that it was an expenditure beyond that contemplated in the By-Laws, and required a two-thirds vote, as provided in Art. II, Sec. 4, of the Constitution. The Grand Chancellor sustained the action of Clay Lodge, whereupon L. appealed to the Grand Lodge, and it sustained the decision of the Grand Chancellor. The facts showed that the money was paid nurses (members of Mystic Lodge, Nevada,) who attended a sick brother and member of Clay Lodge. The by-law was local in its character, and appeared to be designed to operate on sick brothers at home. *Held*, that the decision of the Grand Lodge of Kentucky was wrong, and should be reversed. (*Jour. 1876, 1308.*)

BY–LAWS.
[See Constitution and By-Laws.]

CHANCELLOR COMMANDER.
[See Subordinate Lodges.]

CHARTERS AND DISPENSATIONS.

1. Constitutional provisions: Application for Grand Lodge Charters; Subordinate Lodges.
  2. Of Subordinate Lodges, by whom signed.
  3. Charter must be in Lodge.
  4. Demand to see charter.
  5. Charter annuls dispensation.
  6. Surrender of charter.

[See, also, Delinquent or Defunct Lodges; Grand Lodge; Membership, and Deputy Grand Chancellor (in Grand Lodge); Supreme Lodge; Supreme Chancellor, and Supreme Keeper of Records and Seal (in Supreme Lodge); Subordinate Lodge.]

(1) CONSTITUTIONAL PROVISIONS: APPLICATION FOR GRAND LODGE CHARTERS; SUBORDINATE LODGES.

46. Grand Lodges working under dispensation issued by the Supreme Chancellor must apply in regular course, by petition, for their charter, at the first regular session after their institution, which petition shall be accompanied by their Reports, Constitution, and By-Laws, all of which shall be referred to the proper committees, when, the reports being favorable, and the Committee on Charters and Dispensations reporting and recommending that a charter be issued, and the Supreme Lodge concurring therein, the charter shall then be issued, but not otherwise. (*Const., Art. xx.*)

47. Subordinate Lodges exist by virtue of dispensations issued by the Supreme Lodge through the Supreme Chancellor, or charters granted in lieu thereof, or directly,

2

by the appropriate Grand Lodge; but to each Grand Lodge when formed belongs the exclusive right to issue charters to Lodges instituted within its prescribed territorial jurisdiction. (*Const., Art. viii, Sec. 1.*)

[See Subordinate Lodges.]

(2) CHARTERS OF SUBORDINATE LODGES, BY WHOM SIGNED.

48. The question which set of Grand Lodge officers shall sign the charters for Subordinate Lodges granted immediately before or after the installation of such Grand Officers is of a purely local character, to be settled by the Grand Lodge. (*Jour. 1871, 377, 390; 1870, 209.*)

49. The subject of whose names shall appear upon the charters of the Lodges, when a Grand Lodge has been organized, and upon the surrender of the dispensation, is a subject for local action, and not under the control of the Supreme Chancellor. (*Jour. 1872, 466, 612.*)

(3) CHARTER MUST BE IN LODGE.

50. Neither a Grand nor Subordinate Lodge has a right to work without having its charter or dispensation present in the Lodge or ante-room. (*Jour. 1872, 564, 585; 1873, App. 36.*)

(4) DEMAND TO SEE CHARTER.

51. A Knight in good standing, and evidencing the same to a proper officer or party, may or can ask to see the charter or dispensation of the Lodge, but there is no law or usage warranting a demand; therefore, there being no clandestine organization of our Order, it is optional with the Lodge to exhibit it or not, at its pleasure. (*Jour. 1873, App. 39.*)

(5) CHARTER ANNULS DISPENSATION.

52. The issue of a charter to a Grand Lodge rescinds and annuls any dispensation previously issued, whether said dispensation is returned or not, and all acts done thereafter under such dispensation are illegal. (*Jour. 1873, 714, App. 63.*)

(6) SURRENDER OF CHARTER.

53. No Subordinate Lodge is allowed to dissolve or surrender their charter by their vote so long as nine members remain willing to sustain the Lodge, except by per-mission of the Grand Lodge, or during the recess of the Grand Lodge by the Grand Chancellor of the jurisdiction. (*Jour. 1872, 563, 594.*)

CHARTS.

[See Official Charts.]

COMMITTEES.

1. Of the Supreme Lodge.
2. Relief Committees.

(1) OF THE SUPREME LODGE.

54. The following committees shall be appointed an-nually by the Supreme Chancellor:
Committee on Law and Supervision.
Committee on Finance.
Committee on Appeals and Grievances.
Committee on Credentials and Returns.
Committee on Mileage.
Committee on State of the Order.
Committee on Written Work.
Committee on Unwritten Work.
Committee on Printing.
Committee on Dispensations and Charters. (*Const., Art. v, Sec 1.*)

In addition to the above, in 1871 it was resolved that at the commence-ment of each and every session of the Supreme Lodge, a committee shall be appointed by the Supreme Chancellor, who shall draw for seats to be occupied by the representatives of the several jurisdictions. (*Jour. 1871, 428.*)   [See, also, Rules of Order.]

55. The Committee on Law and Supervision shall, when such subjects are presented to the Supreme Lodge and duly referred to them, inquire into all cases of infrac-tion of the established laws and regulations of the Order, and recommend such measures as they may deem expe-dient for correcting the innovation, and further consider and have charge of all matters coming within the purview of that committee. (*Const., Art. v, Sec. 2.*)

56. At the session of 1873 it was enacted, that on and after that session the various jurisdictions should present their matters of inquiry through the Grand Recording and Corresponding Scribes to the Committee on Law and Supervision at least three weeks before the session of the Supreme Lodge, and that all matters not presented before the assembling of the Supreme Body should be presented at once to the chairman of the Committee on Law and Supervision, and every matter thereafter presented should be subject to pass over to the subsequent session. (*Jour. 1873, 768.*)

57. The **Committee on Finance** shall examine the accounts of the Supreme Master of Exchequer and Supreme Keeper of Records and Seal at each session, and whenever required so to do by the Supreme Lodge. They shall examine and pass upon all bills presented to the Supreme Lodge when in session, and, if correct, report, if approving the same, for economy or creating a remedy by legislation for all extravagant expenditures. They shall make estimates for and recommend appropriations of moneys for general or specific purposes during recess of the Supreme Lodge, and bring down an approximate estimate, based on past results, of the probable revenue likely to accrue; and no expenditures of any character shall be made in excess of the appropriation then made until the next regular session. (*Const., Art. v, Sec. 3.*)

58. The **Committee on Appeals and Grievances** shall hear all appeals and grievances from Grand Lodges or members of Lodges referred to them by the Supreme Lodge, or Supreme Chancellor, and report thereon with the utmost dispatch. (*Const., Art. v, Sec. 4.*)

59. The **Committee on Credentials and Returns** shall examine and report on the returns of the Grand Lodges and Subordinate under the immediate jurisdiction of the Supreme Lodge, and the credentials of all Past Grand Chancellors and Representatives to the Supreme Lodge. (*Const., Art. v, Sec. 5.*)

60. The **Committee on Mileage** shall compute the mileage and per diem of all Supreme Officers and Representatives, at each regular or special called session, making out a proper, complete and accurate roll of the same, and report the amount to which each one on the roll is entitled; and no order shall be drawn for the same until said report is indorsed by a majority of the committee. (*Const., Art. v, Sec. 6.*)

61. The Committee on State of the Order shall examine and report upon such portions of reports of the Supreme Officers and Deputy Supreme Chancellors, so far as the same relate to the state of the Order, and upon such other matters as may be referred to them, presenting in their reports an exhibit of the condition and progress of the Order, and recommending such measures for the good and prosperity of the whole Order as they may think the circumstances require. (*Const., Art. v, Sec. 7.*)

62. The Committee on Written Work shall examine and report upon such parts of reports of the Supreme Officers or other matters referred to them pertaining to all written work of the Order of a public nature, covering regalias, jewels, charts, certificates, shields, uniforms, equipments or public ceremonials, forms for and details of matters not properly of a secret nature. (*Const., Art. v, Sec. 8.*)

63. The Committee on Unwritten Work shall examine and report upon such reports of the Supreme Officers or other matters referred to them of a nature that may be strictly private, or in consonance and keeping with the duties of the name of the committee. (*Const., Art. v, Sec. 9.*)

64. The Committee on Printing shall have general supervisory charge of and examine into all matters referred to or coming within the purview of their duties as suggested by their name; make all contracts not otherwise provided for, compare materials, qualities and price, analyze all bills submitted for printing, binding and supplies, establish a standard style, quality and grade of same, and report their findings and recommendations to the Supreme Lodge. (*Const., Art. v, Sec. 10.*)

[See, also, Jour. 1872, 613; 1873, 741.]

65. The Committee on Dispensations and Charters shall examine into all proper matters referred to them from the Supreme Officers' reports; they shall examine and report on all petitions for warrants of dispensation issued by the Supreme Chancellor for Subordinate or Grand Lodges, or applications for charters for the same, approving or disapproving of the issuing of the same, and other general dispensations, or Deputy Supreme Chancellors' commissions issued during the recess of the Supreme Lodge. (*Const., Art. v, Sec. 11.*)

66. Each of the above named committees shall consist of five members, and when serving on actual work during a recess, by order of the Supreme Lodge or of the Supreme Chancellor, shall have their necessary expenses paid. (*Const., Art. v, Sec. 12.*)

(2) RELIEF COMMITTEES.

67. The question of establishing relief committees is a matter belonging to the local jurisdiction of the Grand Lodges. (*Jour. 1872, 578; 1873, 688, 722.*)

68. In 1875, the Supreme Lodge, by resolution, requested the several Grand Jurisdictions to consider the subject of establishing relief committees in all cities and towns having two or more Subordinate Lodges, for the purpose of relieving transient brethren in distress, and to take such steps toward carrying out the proposed relief system as in their judgment might be deemed consistent and practicable. (*Jour. 1875, 1134, 1142.*)

CONCLAVES.
[See Higher Degrees.]

CONSTITUTION AND BY-LAWS.

1. Old Constitution repealed.
2. Constitution and By-Laws obligatory.
3. Grand and Subordinate Lodge Constitutions.
4. Amendments of Subordinate Lodge Constitution.
5. Amendments of Grand Lodge Constitution.

[See, also, Supreme Lodge; Grand Lodge; Supplies.]

(1) OLD CONSTITUTION REPEALED.

69. The Constitution prior to that adopted at the session of 1874, and all previous legislation inconsistent with the Constitution of 1874, is repealed. (*Jour. 1874, 947.*)

(2) CONSTITUTION AND BY-LAWS OBLIGATORY.

70. All constitutional provisions contained in all Articles, sections or paragraphs of the Constitution and *By-laws* of the Supreme Lodge are obligatory, in every sense, on all Grand and Subordinate Lodges, Knights of Pythias; and all Grand or Subordinate Lodge laws in contravention or conflict herewith are rendered void of effect and illegal in enforcement, or, if enforced, are acts of contumacy liable and subject to proper punishment. (*Const.*, *Art. xiii.*)

(3) GRAND AND SUBORDINATE LODGE CONSTITUTIONS.

71. **Each Grand Lodge** shall adopt a Constitution for its own government, and also a Constitution for its Subordinates, which Constitutions shall be in accordance with the provisions of the Constitution of the Supreme Lodge and the laws made in pursuance thereof. The Constitutions of Grand Lodges, and all amendments thereof, shall not go into effect until submitted to and approved by the Supreme Chancellor or Supreme Lodge. (*Const.*, *Art. vii, Sec. 3.*)

72. **All Grand Lodges** that may have prepared Constitutions for adoption are required to forward the same to the Committee on Laws and Supervision in duplicate copies; and after they shall have been examined and approved by the said committee, one copy shall be returned to the said Grand Lodge, and the other copy shall be retained by the Supreme Scribe in the archives of this Supreme Lodge, to be compared with the printed copies received by him from the said Grand Lodge. (*Jour. 1870, 175.*)

73. **All Grand Lodges** are required to deposit with the Supreme R. and C. S., at their own expense, one printed copy of their Constitution and By-Laws, as soon as possible, for reference by the Supreme Lodge. (*Jour. 1871, 426.*)

Query, whether the two preceding propositions were intended for the particular cases in hand, or to lay down a rule for the future?

74. **A Grand Lodge** cannot, as it seems (under Art. VII, Sec. 3), have *two* Constitutions. (*Jour. 1876, 1288.*)

75. **Grand Lodges** are required to prescribe a Constitution for the Subordinate Lodges within their jurisdiction, containing certain obligatory general rules or principles. (*Const.*, *Art. viii, Sec. 2; Jour. 1869, 115.*)

As these general rules are diverse in their character, they have been distributed throughout the work where they respectively belong, and when laying down any rule, are marked " Obligatory," to designate their character as per above clause.

76. **The obligatory passages** of the old Constitution

for Subordinate Lodges were held to apply to all Subordinate Lodges, whether under the immediate jurisdiction of the Supreme or a Grand Lodge. (*Jour. 1872, 579.*)

The meaning of the term obligatory under the old Constitution was defined in the following resolution: " That the provisions of the laws of the Supreme Lodge relating to the Constitutions of Grand and Subordinate Lodges to the effect that matter italicized is obligatory, mean simply that those bodies have no option as to accepting them, but do not mean that said italicized words must be printed in their Constitutions." (*Jour. 1873, 699, 734.*)

(4) AMENDMENTS OF SUPREME LODGE CONSTITUTION.

77. No alteration or amendment to the Constitution of the Supreme Lodge shall be made unless presented at a regular session, and adopted by a two-thirds vote at the next succeeding regular session: *Provided*, that no change shall be made in the Written or Unwritten Work unless the same lay over from one session to another, nor then unless four-fifths of the representatives concur therein. (*Const., Art. xxxiii.*)

Under the old Constitution Grand Lodges had the power of amending the Subordinate Lodge Constitution at any regular session. (*Jour. 1872, 587.*)

(5) AMENDMENTS OF GRAND LODGE CONSTITUTION.

78. It is a fatal objection to the approval of an insurance scheme presented as an amendment of the Constitution of a State Grand Lodge, that it provides that it " may be amended by a two-thirds vote of all the members present of the Board of Directors at the annual meeting of the board," etc., because the effect of it would be to take a part of the Constitution of the Grand Lodge from the control of the Grand Lodge, to which it is entitled under Sec. 2, Art. VII, of the Supreme Lodge Constitution. (*Jour. 1876, 1289, 1290.*)

CREDENTIALS.
[See Supreme Lodge; Withdrawal Cards.]

DEDICATION CEREMONY.

79. In 1871 a new form of dedication ceremony, retaining the former ceremony used, with additional prefatory matter, was adopted for general use by the Supreme, Grand

and Subordinate Bodies, which may be given in public when so desired. *(Jour. 1870, 229; 1871, 364, 385.)*

DEGREES.
[See Higher Degrees ; Ritual ; Rank.]

DELINQUENT OR DEFUNCT LODGES.
[See Appeals.]

80. Any Grand or Subordinate Lodge may be suspended or dissolved, and its charter or dispensation forfeited to the Supreme or the proper Grand Lodge —

1. For improper conduct.

2. For neglecting or refusing to conform to the Constitution, Laws or Enactments of the Supreme or its Grand Lodge, or the general laws and regulations of the Order.

3. For neglecting or refusing to make its returns, or for non-payment of dues or taxes to the Supreme or its proper Grand Lodge. But the charter or dispensation shall not be forfeited in either of the above cases until the Lodge shall have been duly notified of its offense by the Supreme or proper Grand Keeper of Records and Seal, and suitable opportunity given to answer the charges made against it.

4. For neglecting to hold the regular stated meetings as provided by law, without a proper dispensation therefor, or unless prevented from doing so by some unforeseen circumstance.

5. By its membership diminishing, so that less than a constitutional quorum may be left. *(Const., Art. viii, Sec. 3.)*

DEPUTY SUPREME CHANCELLOR.
[See Supreme Lodge, etc.]

DISPENSATIONS.
[See Charters.]

DUES.

1. One year in arrears.
2. Who liable for.
3. Exemption from.
4. May be required in advance.

(1) One Year in Arrears.

[See, also, Membership. Delinquent or Defunct Lodges ; Installation ; Offenses ; Official Receipt.]

81. A member who is one year in arrears shall be declared suspended, provided said member is not under charges. [Obligatory.] (*Const. Art. viii, Sec. 2.*)

82. By the expression, "One year in arrears," found in paragraph 21, Sec. 2, Art. VIII, S. L. Const., it was intended to declare that a member owing for twelve months' dues should be declared suspended; and it is not necessary where the dues are payable quarterly to wait till the expiration of fifteen months. (*Jour. 1876, 1232, 1302.*)

83. Under Art. IX [old] Subordinate Lodge Constitution, which read as follows—"Each Subordinate Lodge shall regulate its dues and benefits; provided, however, that a member who is one year in arrears shall stand suspended"—a member could not be suspended until he was one year in arrears. (*Jour. 1872, 531, 585.*)

84. The length of time a member may be in arrears for dues before he can be deprived of the S. A. P. W., is a question subject to the legislation of State Grand Bodies so long as said jurisdictions comply with the requirement of this Supreme Body by suspending members who are twelve months in arrears for dues. (*Jour. 1872, 466, 468, 613, 614; 1875, 1121.*)

85. When a member is twelve months in arrears he should be notified thereof, and the fact of his suspension declared by the Chancellor Commander in open Lodge, and a record thereof made on the minutes. (*Jour. 1876, 1232, 1302.*) See, however, *Jour. 1872, 595,* where it is said that the manner of suspending a member for non-payment of dues belongs to the local jurisdictions.

86. "Arrears for one year" does not mean dues, fines and assessments, which, added together, would equal the amount of weekly dues for one year. (*Jour. 1873, 768.*)

87. And a Lodge cannot by its By-Laws, approved by the Grand Lodge and Grand Chancellor, declare that a member owing for funeral assessments, fines, etc., an amount equal to one year's dues, is liable to suspension. (*Jour. 1876, 1284, 1296, 1300.*)

(2) Who Liable for.

88. The charging of and collecting dues from Pages and Esquires rests solely with Subordinate Lodges. (*Jour. 1873, App. 37.*)

89. In 1872 the Supreme Chancellor decided that Pages and Esquires ought not to be charged dues, they not being entitled to all rights, privileges and advantages until they become Knights, and fully instructed. (*Jour. 1871, 327, 335; 1872, 465, 468; see, also, p. 612.*) When the subject came before the Supreme Lodge on the question of sustaining the minority report of the committee in favor of the ruling, the point of order was made that the Supreme Lodge could not interfere with the Grand Lodges with reference to dues and benefits of Subordinate Lodges, and the point of order was by the Supreme Chancellor decided to have been well taken, which decision was affirmed by the Supreme Lodge. (*Jour. 1872, 614.*)

90. Since the decision of the Supreme Chancellor in 1870, relative to parties suspended for non-payment of dues, it is not lawful (unless under the provisions of local constitutional enactments) to charge parties so suspended with dues, after the act of suspension, until reinstated. (*Jour. 1875, 1112, 1156.*)

91. A member who is under charges cannot, when under charges, be declared suspended for non-payment of dues. (*Jour. 1875, 1112, 1156.*)

(3) Exemption from.

92. A Lodge cannot make a law exempting all new members from the payment of dues for six months after being enrolled as Knights, since this would not be consistent with the laws or usages of the Order. (*Jour. 1876, 1128, 1296.*)

(4) May be Required in Advance.

93. A Subordinate Lodge may collect dues in advance; but cannot declare a member in arrears for dues who has paid the same to the first of a term, or allow the advanced payment required, to invalidate the member's right to benefits or the S. A. P. W. (*Jour. 1875, 1042, 1121.*)

ELECTIONS AND APPOINTMENTS.

1. In Supreme Lodge.
2. In Subordinate Lodge.

[See, also. Grand Lodge ; Supreme Lodge and Officers ; Ritual ; Nominations.]

(1) IN SUPREME LODGE.

94. The Supreme Lodge Officers shall be elected bi-annually by ballot. A majority of all the votes present shall be necessary to constitute a choice. In case of a tie, the balloting shall continue until a choice is made; the name of the brother receiving the lowest number of votes at each balloting shall be withdrawn. Any officer who may be absent at the time of installation, unless excused by the Supreme Lodge, or by sickness, his office shall be declared vacant, and another and immediate election held to fill the vacancy. But if the absent officer elect has been excused, or is ill, then the Supreme Chancellor may be empowered to install during recess, at his convenience. (*Const., Art. xxviii.*)

95. Where there is but one nominee for an office in the Supreme Lodge, it is competent for that body to designate a member to cast the ballot of the Supreme Lodge. (*Jour. 1870, 194, 195; 1876, 1269, 1270.*)

96. But in such a case all members voting against the motion to designate a member to cast the vote of the Supreme Lodge, have an inherent right to vote with such member. (*Jour. 1870, 195.*)

97. And in such case all the ballots being cast for the same person, it is the unanimous vote of the Supreme Lodge, although all of the members do not vote. (*Jour. 1870, 196.*)

(2) IN SUBORDINATE LODGE.

[See Vacancies.]

98. The C. C., V. C., P., K. of R. and S., M. of F., and M. of E., *must* be elected by ballot. The M. at A. may be elected or appointed; the I. G., O. G., and attendants *must* be appointed. (*Jour. 1875, 1043, 1114.*)

[See Jour. 1873, 768.]

99. In the formation of a Subordinate Lodge the office

of V. P.* is filled by selection of the charter members at the institution of the Lodge. (*Jour. 1872, 620, 630.*)

* This would now apply to the P. C.

EMBLEMS.

[See Uniform, etc.]

ESQUIRES.

[See Rank; Dues.]

FEES.

[See Membership.]

FINES.

[See Benefits.]

FLAG.

[See Banner.]

FOREIGN COUNTRIES.

100. The Supreme Chancellor may authorize and establish the Order in foreign countries, arrange for and assent to the institution of Grand Lodges therein, under proper reservations for mutual advantage; but, in all instances, exacting and holding intact the spirit, letter and intent of this Constitution and By-Laws. (*Const., Art. xvii.*)

101. The Supreme Chancellor was in 1875 instructed to give his special attention to all opportunities that might present themselves for extending the Order in all parts of the habitable globe; and that if, in his judgment, this end could be accomplished by the appointment of properly qualified agents in any part of the world, keeping in view the condition of the finances in regard to all expenses incurred, he was instructed to so appoint such agents or deputies. (*Jour. 1875, 1142 ; re-affirmed in 1876, in Jour. 1876, 1274.*)

FOUNDER OF THE ORDER.

102. At the first session of the Supreme Lodge in 1868, Justus H. Rathbone was duly elected Founder and Past

Supreme Chancellor, a rank which dies with that officer. (*Jour. 1868, 13.*)   See, also, Jour. 1876, 1277, 1278, where Justus H. Rathbone was fully recognized by the Supreme Lodge as Sole Founder of the Order of Knights of Pythias.

FUNERALS.

[See Funeral Rosette, in Uniform, Regalia, etc.]

103. When the Order attends funerals, the line of march shall be taken up in the following order:

First — O. G., bearing a sword, followed by the Pages, Esquires and Knights in the order as laid down.

Second — I. G., bearing a sword.

Third — K. of R. and S., M. of F., and M. of E. (three abreast), each bearing the emblems of their respective offices.

Fourth — M. A. A., bearing a staff.

Fifth — C. C. and V. C., each bearing the emblems of their respective offices.

Sixth — P., supported by two P. Cs.

Seventh — P. Cs. and P. G. Cs.

On arriving at the grave the procession halts and opens order, when the coffin and mourners pass through, and the procession follows the corpse in a reversed position. (*Jour. 1871, 403, 414.*)

104. In 1872 the word "kneel," wherever occurring in the Funeral Services or Ritual, except in the ceremonies of the First Degree, was stricken out, and the word "stand" or "standing" inserted in its or their places. (*Jour. 1872, 599.*)

105. Subordinate Lodges have the power to elect, or their presiding officers may appoint, a Chaplain to conduct the devotional exercises at funerals of members of the Order. (*Jour. 1872, 563, 598.*)

GERMAN D. D. G. C.
[See Honors.]

GIFT ENTERPRISES.
[See Lotteries.]

GRAND LODGES AND THEIR OFFICERS.

1. Mode of forming.
2. Composition of.
3. Powers and duties of Grand Lodges.
4. Revocation of charters.
5. Grand Lodge officers.
6. Sessions.

[See Reports ; Incorporation ; Offenses ; Charters : Supreme Lodge; Uniform, and Condition of Admission under Uniform.]

(1) MODE OF FORMING.

106. When there are five or more Subordinate Lodges, established and in working order in any jurisdiction, they, through the Deputy Supreme Chancellor thereof, may petition the Supreme Chancellor, who shall cause the Supreme K. of R. and S. to notify each of the Lodges of that jurisdiction to elect two representatives for the unexpired balance of the year, up to the 31st day of December following, on the first meeting night of the Lodge after the receipt of the communication. (*Const., Art. vi, Sec. 2.*)

107. The Past Chancellors of the five or more Lodges, together with the representatives elect, shall meet at such place as may be specified by the Supreme Chancellor, and proceed to organize a Grand Lodge by electing a Past Grand Chancellor, Grand Chancellor, Grand Vice Chancellor, Grand Prelate, Grand Master of Exchequer, Grand Keeper of Records and Seal, Grand Master-at-Arms, Grand Inner Guard, Grand Outer Guard, all of whom must be Past Chancellors. (*Const., Art. vi, Sec. 3.*)

108. A re-elected and installed C. C. is eligible, after his second installation, to be elected as representative, unless disqualified by some local law. (*Jour. 1875, 1114.*)

109. A Grand Lodge charter cannot constitutionally be granted where there are only three Subordinate Lodges in the State sought to be made a Grand Lodge Jurisdiction. (*Jour. 1875, 1156.*)

110. Where the petition and papers for the establishment of a new Grand Lodge in a portion of a State already under the jurisdiction of the Grand Lodge of such State, did not show clearly that the petition came from Lodges as such, and it did not come through the State Grand Lodge, nor by its consent; *held*, that the matter was not properly before the Supreme Lodge for action. (*Jour. 1875, 1148.*)

111. **The Grand Lodge,** as soon as organized, shall elect two representatives to the Supreme Lodge, as prescribed in Sec. 2, Art. II, of the Constitution, and the said representatives are hereby declared Past Grand Chancellors. (*Const., Art. vi, Sec. 4.*)

112. **A notice** of their organization, together with a list of their officers, shall be forwarded to the Supreme K. of R. and S. through the Supreme Chancellor, and the latter officer shall install, or cause to be installed, by a Deputy Supreme Chancellor, the officers elect of said Grand Lodge, after which it shall proceed to frame a Constitution and By-Laws for its own government, not inconsistent with the laws promulgated by this body. (*Const., Art. vi, Sec. 5.*)

(2) COMPOSITION OF.

113. **Grand Lodges** shall be composed only of Past Chancellors, but said Grand Lodges may provide for a representative system, and may limit the rights and privileges of Past Chancellors on the floor of the Grand Lodge. (*Const., Art. vii, Sec. 4.*)

This would imply that Supreme Representatives *are not* officers, and if not officers, would not, in Grand Lodges where the representative system prevails and representatives and officers only are permitted to vote or speak, have any more privileges than a Past Chancellor. Under the old Constitution they were officers.

114. **The officers** of a Grand Lodge shall be as prescribed in Sec. 3 of Art. VI of this Constitution, who shall be elected or appointed as the Constitutions of the respective Grand Lodges may prescribe, and who shall hold office for the term of one year. (*Const., Art. vii, Sec. 5.*)

(3) POWERS AND DUTIES OF GRAND LODGES.

115. **Grand Lodges** exist by virtue of a charter or dispensation issued by authority of the Supreme Lodge, or Supreme Chancellor during its recess. They shall conform to the Ritual, Forms, Ceremonies, Work, Regalia, Jewels, Uniform, Charts, Shields and Certificates, and regulations prescribed by the Supreme Lodge, in accordance with this Constitution, and shall (subject to the provisions hereof and

right of appeal) have exclusive original jurisdiction over all Subordinate Lodges within their territorial limit, and over the members attached to the same. (*Const., Art. vii, Sec. 1.*)

116. All power and authority not herein reserved to the Supreme Lodge is hereby delegated to the Grand Lodges; the Supreme Lodge, however, reserving to itself the right at any time, by proper amendments, duly adopted, to this Constitution, to resume any additional power necessary to promote the well-being and harmony of the Order. (*Const., Art. vii, Sec. 2.*)

117. The Grand Lodge holds jurisdiction over its members, and when charged *as such* all laws operative there or below are applicable until the matter is fully determined. (*Jour. 1873, App. 37.*)

This ruling is given because it *is* a ruling. It is classed under the caption of Grand Lodges because *if it refers to anything* it does to them. As a ruling, it would be a " handy thing to have " in a Grand Chancellor's office, for use when nothing else known would appear applicable, as it would seem sufficiently ambiguous to mean anything or nothing.

118. Extra territorial jurisdiction by constitutional grant has always been refused to Grand Lodges by the Supreme Lodge. (*Jour. 1876, 1310.*)

[See Subordinate Lodges.]

119. A Grand Lodge is competent to confer upon such Knights as are duly recommended to it by its Subordinate Lodges, the degree of Past Chancellor. (*Jour. 1870, 199.*)

120. It is the duty of a Grand Lodge to receive a protest from its Grand Chancellor, when no misstatements, disrespect or unfairness are contained therein. (*Jour. 1870, 199.*)

121. The legal method of communication from the Supreme Authority to the Subordinate Lodges of the several jurisdictions where Grand Lodges have been instituted is through the Grand Lodge. (*Jour. 1872, 618, 630.*)

(4) REVOCATION OF CHARTERS OF.

[See Offenses.]

122. Charters of Grand Lodges may be revoked, and Grand Lodges suspended, by the Supreme Lodge, for nonconformity to the Work, Ceremonies or Ritual adopted by the Supreme Lodge; for disobedience to its legal mandates, and for improper conduct. (*Const., Art. vii, Sec. 6.*)

123. Where a State Grand Lodge has been suspended for insubordination, and a new loyal Grand Lodge instituted and recognized by the Supreme Lodge, the status of the members of the suspended Grand Lodge, and the manner in which they can regain membership in the Order, is under the control of the Grand Lodge of the State, which is recog-- nized by this Supreme Lodge. (*Jour. 1871, 428.*)

(5) Grand Lodge Officers.
[See *ante*, (1) (2)]

124. The officers of the Grand Lodge, who are not representatives to the same, have the right to vote upon all questions that may arise before the Grand Lodge. (*Jour. 1871, 361, 391.*)

Past Grand Chancellor.
[See Supreme Lodge ; Vacancies.]

125. The customary and proper mode of attaining the rank of Past Grand Chancellor is by service in the chair of Grand Chancellor; and in 1875 the Supreme Lodge declared it inexpedient to provide any other method of attaining that rank. (*Jour. 1875, 1152.*)

126. The retiring Grand Chancellor of each Grand Lodge shall become a Past Grand Chancellor without any regard to the length of time he has served in that office. (*Jour. 1868, 55.*)

127. The rule formerly was, First — That to give the color of the Past-official rank of Past Grand Chancellor, the habitant of the Grand Chancellor's chair must be present and be officially passed to his proper or the Past Grand Chancellor's chair prior to even being entitled to the prefix of Past Grand Chancellor or title. (*Jour. 1873, 710, 735; 1874, 845; 1875, 1034.*)

Second — That the Past Grand Chancellor was an officer of the Grand Lodge, and only became fully entitled to the title of Past Grand Chancellor at the expiration of his term as that officer; that while virtually so by process of advancement, was not actually so until serving his full term as Past Grand Chancellor. (*Jour. 1874, 845; 1875, 1034.*)

Third — That while having those present who had gone forward and received the full rank of Past Grand Chancellor in the Supreme Lodge, or served their *full* time as Past Grand Chancellor, the passing Grand Chancellor and the acting Past Grand Chancellor *was not eligible for Supreme Representative so long as those fully qualified would accept of it;* and more especially so when the outgoing Grand Chancellor was not present even to be passed to the Past Grand Chancellor's chair. (*Jour. 1874, 845; 1875, 1034.*)

But at the session of the Supreme Lodge in 1875 it was enacted —

That thereafter any Grand Chancellor, who has served a full term in that office, and against whom no charges are pending, shall be entitled to the rank and title of Past Grand Chancellor as soon as his successor is installed.

That a Grand Chancellor, on being reëlected, shall be entitled to the rank and title of Past Grand Chancellor immediately after his second installation. (*Jour. 1875, 1035.*)

That no one is eligible to election as Supreme Representative until he is entitled to the rank and title of Past Grand Chancellor. (*Jour. 1873, 710, 735; 1875, 1035, 1113; 1876, 1267.*)

128. Since the adoption of the Constitution of 1874, there is no authority for a Grand Lodge to elect a Past Grand Chancellor. Although there is no express, there is an implied, prohibition of such action; and as a general provision there is not only propriety but a necessity, so far as the same is practicable, to keep the honors that are coupled with past services strictly within and confined to those that have performed the services for the constitutional period. (*Jour. 1876, 1286, 1287.*)

[See contra, Jour. 1869, 99.]

129. And where the Grand Chancellor of Indiana died pending his term, and the duties of the office devolved upon and were performed by the Grand Vice Chancellor, for the balance of the term, who at the next annual session of the Grand Lodge of that State was duly elected Grand Chancellor, leaving the office of Past Grand Chancellor vacant, whereupon the Grand Lodge proceeded to elect M. a Past Grand Chancellor to supply the vacancy for the ensuing year, it was considered that although M. was not legally entitled to the rank of Past Grand Chancellor (*Jour. 1876, 1276*), yet in view of the peculiar circumstances the State Jurisdiction was justified in the election of M., and the rank of Past Grand Chancellor was conferred upon him by the Supreme Lodge. (*Jour. 1876, 1276, 1283, 1286.*)

130. And the same rule has been applied to the case of the resignation of the Grand Chancellor. (*Jour. 1876, 1287, 1298.*)

131. Where a Grand Chancellor is reëlected, the Grand Lodge has no right to elect a Grand Ven. Patriarch, as the then Grand Ven. Patriarch holds over and retains his position for another term. (*Jour. 1871, 380, 392.*)

[See, also, Vacancies.]

132. It is in the power of the Supreme Lodge to confer the rank of Past Grand Chancellor for meritorious services. (*Jour. 1875, 1156.*)

GRAND CHANCELLOR.

133. The law, making only a Past Vice-Grand Chancellor or a Past Grand Chancellor eligible to the position of Grand Chancellor, and all legislation on the same subject prior to the adoption of this repealing enactment, was repealed in 1871. (*Jour. 1871, 389, 417.*)

134. Prior to the passage of the legislation in the next preceding section it was held that where a vacancy occurs in the office of Grand Chancellor, the Vice-Grand Chancellor is the proper officer to succeed him, and he cannot be superseded by the election of another over him. (*Jour. 1868, 26, 71, 86, 106; 1870, 140.*)

135. The Grand Chancellor or his deputy may give instruction in the secret work outside of the Lodge room, and may also give the S. A. P. W. to a Chancellor Commander. (*Jour. 1873, 724.*)

(6) SESSIONS.

136. The Grand Lodges of the various jurisdictions have ample power to determine when and how often they will hold their sessions. (*Jour. 1871, 394.*)

137. A Grand Lodge has power to amend its constitution so as to dispense with semi-annual sessions. (*Jour. 1870, 201, 202.*)

138. By Sec. 3, Art. II, of the new Constitution of the Grand Lodge of Pennsylvania, "business of a *local* character" is to be transacted at the semi-annual session in February, "but all business of a *general* character, affecting the interests of Subordinate Lodges throughout the State, or amendments to the laws of Grand or Subordinate Lodges, if offered, shall be entered upon the Journal, the Lodges duly notified, and *action on the same postponed until the next annual session.*" At the session of said Grand Lodge in February, 1874, charges and specifications having been preferred against G. C. W. J. M., a resolution was adopted ordering him to vacate the position of Grand Chancellor, and that the Vice-Grand Chancellor act as Grand Chancellor until the annual session in August, which resolution was insisted by W. J. M. to be business of a general character, and in violation of the constitutional provision above quoted: *Held*, that such a construction of said constitutional provision would be altogether too strict and close, and that such action was not in violation of that provision. (*Jour. 1875, 1127.*)

139. Where a special meeting of a Grand Lodge was called by the Grand Chancellor fixing time, place, and business to be transacted, and the Grand Chancellor being absent from the session a Past Grand Chancellor was called to preside, and after the transaction of some business a paper was circulated and signed by five Past Chancellors requesting the call of another special session of the Grand Lodge, and the then presiding officer adjourned the session called by the Grand Chancellor, and immediately opened a session of that body, calling it a special session of such Grand Lodge, and proceeded to the transaction of business: *Held*, that such pretended special session was illegal, and all its proceedings null and void. (*Jour. 1869, 71, 106.*)

HIGHER DEGREES; CONCLAVES, Etc.

1. No higher degrees.
2. Conclaves; O. B. N.
[See Ritual.]

(1) NO HIGHER DEGREES.

140. There are no higher degrees of the Order than those established in its Ritual. (*Jour. 1868, 17, 43, 44.*)

Many unsuccessful efforts have been made to change this legislation.

The following resolution (Jour. 1876, 1283) bearing on the subject was not even referred, but was unceremoniously " laid on the table ":

"*Resolved*, That there be immediate steps taken to organize. under the jurisdiction and control of the Supreme Lodge, a higher body with a proper ritual, regalia, uniform, written and unwritten work, etc.; and that a special committee of five be appointed for that purpose. to report at the next session of this body."

(2) CONCLAVES OF S. P. K. ; O. B. N.

141. The subject of Conclaves of S. P. K. (claiming to be a higher degree of the Order) in the earlier years of the Supreme Lodge proved a fruitful source of difficulty.   The legislation by which its progress was checked and the so-called Order abolished is as follows:

At the session of 1868 the action had upon the subject of Conclaves was in substance that the so-called Order of S. P. K. is no part of the Order of Knights of Pythias, and members of the Order should have no connection therewith.   (*Jour. 1868, 27, 43, 44, 45, 47, 59.*)

142. At the session of 1869 the Supreme Lodge assumed the control and government of all so-called "Conclaves" of S. P. K., and placed the same in charge of a committee, . with full power to do all things requisite to protect the rights, privileges and prerogatives of said Conclaves, or brothers connected therewith, and the welfare and interest of the Order of K. of P.; with directions that no new Conclaves be chartered or created till the next session of the Supreme Lodge, and that said degrees be not conferred outside of a regular Conclave. (*Jour. 1869, 114.*)

143. At the session of 1870, this legislation being found inadequate, the following resolutions were adopted:

"*Resolved*, that all Past Chancellors, members of this Order, who are attached to the Order known as S. P. K., or Conclaves, are hereby required to present to their respective Grand Lodges conclusive evidence, within sixty days, that they have purged themselves of all connection with the Order of S. P. K., or Conclaves of said Order; and in the event of their failure to do so, the several Grand Lodges be, and they are hereby ordered and directed to refuse all such brothers admittance, and all officers who are members of Grand Lodges refusing compliance shall be forthwith removed from office.

"*Resolved*, That all Grand Chancellors, except the Grand Chancellor of the State of Maryland, shall forward all such evidence to this Supreme Lodge.

The Supreme Chancellor was directed to cite the Past Grand Chancellor of Maryland before the Committee on Conclaves, and require of him such evidence of his disconnection with the Conclaves of S. P. K. as should convince him that he had purged himself of his offense.

"*Resolved*, That all members of the Supreme Lodge who are members of the Conclaves of S. P. K., who fail to furnish such evidence to their Grand Lodges within the time specified for transmission to this Supreme Lodge be and are hereby declared forever disqualified from taking a seat in this body as a member thereof.

"*Resolved*, That any member of this Order who is now in affiliation with the Conclaves of S. P. K. shall immediately dissolve all connection with said organization.

"*Resolved*, That every member who may refuse to abjure his connection with Conclaves of S. P. K. shall be suspended by the Lodge to which he may be attached.

"*Resolved*, That the several Grand Lodges be directed to enforce the above resolutions, and any Lodge that may refuse to obey the mandates of this Supreme Lodge shall forfeit its charter." (*Jour. 1870, 217, 218.*)

144. At the same session (1870) it was also "*Resolved*, That any and all action had by this Supreme Lodge on the subject-matter of 'S. P. K.' or Conclaves, shall not in any manner be taken, accepted or admitted as recognizing in *any* sense the existence of said bodies, or coloring of legality as emanating from this body; and that all Conclaves of S. P. K., and any organization springing therefrom, are herewith emphatically repudiated, and are considered as an injury to this Order, and detrimental to the peace and harmony of this Supreme Lodge, and the several jurisdictions working under said Supreme Lodge." (*Jour. 1870, 225.*)

145. At the session of 1871 the construction of the "O. B. N." was settled by resolution as meaning: "No other body, association or organization of any kind whatsoever, other than the Conclaves, of S. P. K.—and they only so long as claiming to be a higher degree of the Pythian Order, and no longer." (*Jour. 1871, 304, 365, 396.*)

On page 396 of the Journal of 1871 it is stated that the report of the committee recommending the adoption of Doc. 25, p. 365, was adopted, while lower down on the same page the same recommendation is repeated, and it is stated to have been referred to the secret session.

146. **The legislation** had in 1871 for the purpose of completing the legislation as had and made on the matter of enforcing the legislation of this Supreme Body at that session, covering the application of the qualified O. B. N., is as follows:

The Supreme Lodge created and invested its Supreme Chancellor and Officers with the following extraordinary powers, to be exercised and used during the vacation of the Supreme Body, viz.:

The right and power again, and for the last time, to *order* the *immediate* conforming to and with the present legislation of the Supreme Body within a given space of time, of not less than thirty days nor exceeding six months from date of issuance of their said order.

That proper evidences of said action of conformity in letter and spirit shall be furnished them by all to whom their said order may be directed, within the time therein specified, as also the steps taken for its proper enforcement, and its results.

That in case of any Grand Jurisdiction, either through its Grand Lodge action, or in its vacation, the Grand Officers thereof, refusing to, or in a spirit of contumacy attempting to intervene and prevent its being conformed to, the proper Supreme authority may declare the charter or charters of said contumacious Grand Lodges arrested, suspended, and forfeited, and promulgate said fact to the loyal Grand Jurisdictions for publication.

Immediately upon the declaration and promulgation of said order of arrest and forfeiture of the charter of any non-conforming Grand Lodge, the proper Supreme authority shall enter said jurisdiction by its proper representatives and D. G. Cs. and proceed to collect around it the loyal element that may be therein, and, if sufficient in numbers, under the law take the initiatory steps to, and form a new Grand Lodge under dispensation until granted a charter in regular course in this Supreme Body, to replace the one arrested and forfeited by the act of non-conformity of the old Grand Lodge.

That immediately after the arrest and suspension of the charter or charters of any and all non-conforming or disloyal Grand Lodges, the spiritual or actual control of all Subordinate Lodges in those said contumacious and non-conforming former jurisdictions shall revert to, and be exclusively within and under, the control of the representatives and proper D. G. Cs. of the Supreme Body until a Grand Lodge shall be established; and any Subordinate Lodge, or element therein, refusing to recognize, acknowledge and conform to the specific legislation of the Supreme Body, as properly promulgated through them, shall be declared suspended, their charters forfeited, and their membership excluded from *all* loyal Lodges, until yielding obedience and conformity to the laws of the Supreme Body through its properly delegated and recognized authority and officers, or healed by and under proper legislation of the new Grand Lodge that may be instituted and recognized by the Supreme Body as existing therein.

That all necessary steps shall be taken by the proper Supreme authority, D. G. Cs. and the new Grand Lodges to promulgate the names, numbers and locations of conforming and *non*-conforming Subordinate Lodges, that those who refuse to obey the lawful mandates and legislation of the Supreme Body may be excluded from entrance into or the privileges of all loyal Lodges wherever existing, and that said roster of Lodges shall be kept fully up to and cover the names of all regular, law-abiding and conforming Grand and Subordinate Lodges, and fully promulgated through all Grand Lodges and jurisdictions that are loyal to and conforming with the laws and edicts of this Supreme Body.

Any and all necessary legal and proper steps that present themselves in any exigencies that may arise, and that are not herein and before specifically mentioned and set forth, be and the same are hereby delegated to the proper Supreme Officers of this Supreme Body for proper and *stringent* enforcement of and requirement with the mandates, laws and legislation of the Supreme Body, and that said Supreme Officers, their representatives and D. G. Cs. shall make full and complete reports of their acts and measures done and prosecuted to and for the objects intended and desired, with the results thereof, to the Supreme Body, for its final examination and approval. (*Jour. 1871, 419-421.*)

147. As a measure of relief to members of Subordinate

Lodges improperly suspended on that occasion, the following was enacted:

"WHEREAS, This Supreme Lodge is advised that members of the Order of K. of P. have been suspended in their Subordinate Lodges, in various jurisdictions, for the alleged offense of having complied with the mandates of the Supreme Lodge in subscribing to the so-called O. B. N.; therefore be it

"*Resolved*, That all Subordinate Lodges having suspended any member or members for the reason above assigned, be and they are hereby directed forthwith to reinstate to full rights and privileges of membership any member or members, so suspended; and no Lodge shall be permitted to enforce the payment of any dues or penalties during the continuance of said suspension.

"*Resolved*, That the several Grand Lodges be and they are hereby directed to carry the above resolution into effect." (*Jour. 1871, 427.*)

148. On the appeal of Nonpareil Lodge, No. 11, from the decision of the Grand Lodge of New Jersey, in the suspension and conditions of reinstating said Lodge, which appeal grew out of the enforcement of the so-called O. B. N. case, the facts were as follows: In 1870 the Grand Chancellor suspended Nonpareil Lodge, No. 11, for non-compliance with the law enforcing said O. B. N. Charges were preferred against said Lodge, and notices given the Lodge of same. The Lodge did not appear to answer to said charges, and the Grand Lodge suspended said Lodge for contempt. Following the session of this Supreme Lodge of 1871, Nonpareil Lodge made inquiry of the Grand Chancellor on what terms or conditions they could be reinstated. The Grand Chancellor replied in substance: 1st, Full compliance with the O. B. N. in its present form, and the law enforcing the same; 2d, that the Lodge be reinstated as existing at the time of suspension; 3d, that all persons initiated during the suspension of the Lodge cannot be recognized in any way as members of the Order. *Held*, by the Supreme Lodge, that the Grand Lodge of New Jersey should propose to Nonpareil Lodge, No. 11, the following conditions of reinstatement: 1st, That said Lodge, as existing on the 28th day of May, 1870, shall be recognized as *the Lodge* to be reinstated when such members and said Lodge shall fully comply with the law of [and] O. B. N. as now in force, and shall make payment in full of their indebtedness to the Grand Lodge at time of suspension; 2d, That all persons initiated during the suspension of said Lodge may be received as members by each being obligated in each degree, after said Lodge has been duly reinstated. (*Jour. 1872, 567, 608.*)

HONORS.

1. Deputy Supreme Chancellor.
2. Promotions, etc.

[See Vacancies.]

(1) DEPUTY SUPREME CHANCELLOR.

149. Any Knight to whom a commission as Deputy Supreme Chancellor shall be issued, in any State, country, territory or island, where the Order is not already established, or if so, where no Grand Lodge exists, shall be entitled to, and receive the rank of Past Chancellor; and if in a territory where the Order exist, and a Grand Lodge is instituted while he is in charge thereof, he shall be entitled to, and receive at the hands of this Supreme Lodge, the rank and grade of Past Grand Chancellor therefor. Except as above, or as otherwise provided in this Constitution, the grade or rank of Past Grand Chancellor shall not be conferred upon any Past Chancellor who has not served as Grand Chancellor: *Provided*, that German District Deputy Grand Chancellors, whose jurisdiction is coëxtensive with their State, who have been elected or appointed by the Grand Lodge, and who serve for three successive years, shall be entitled to the rank of Past Grand Chancellor. (*Const., Art. 21.*)

[See Jour. 1872, 581, 592; also, Past Grand Chancellor.]

150. No legislation is necessary to carry into effect the legislation that any Past Chancellor serving as German District Deputy Grand Chancellor, for the term of three years, shall be entitled to the rank of Past Grand Chancellor; but upon the presentation by the applicant of the proper certificates and proofs that he has complied with the requisitions of the section entitled "German Deputies," passed at the session of 1872, the rank prayed for will be conferred upon him. (*Jour. 1874, 933.*)

(2) Promotions, etc.

151. Any officer can be promoted and retain the honors of his former office. (*Jour. 1872, 564, 585.*)

152. The honors of the same office cannot be given to but one person for the same term. (*Jour. 1872, 585.*)

I suppose that by the above, which is quoted *literally*, it is meant that the honors of the same office can be given to but one person for the same term, as otherwise it involves the absurd proposition that such honors cannot be given to one person, but must be conferred on more than one.

153. A Vice Chancellor can act as Chancellor Commander during his term as Vice Chancellor, but cannot receive the honors. (*Jour. 1872, 564, 585.*)

154. P. C. A. was Grand Vice Chancellor, and after the resignation of the Grand Chancellor performed the duties of Grand Chancellor, but was not elected to that office. *Held,* that while the laws of the Order confer upon the Vice-Grand Chancellor the duties and powers of Grand Chancellor during the absence or in case of removal or death of the Grand Chancellor for the time being, they do not confer upon him the honors of the office; and that A. was not entitled to the degree or rank of Past Grand Chancellor, but ranked as Past Vice-Grand Chancellor only. (*Jour. 1871, 340.*)

INCORPORATION.

1. Of Supreme Lodge.
2. Of Grand and Subordinate Lodges.

[See Board of Trustees.]

(1) Certificate of Association of the Supreme Lodge of Knights of Pythias.

155. Whereas, It is deemed advisable to have the Supreme Lodge of Knights of Pythias an incorporated body, under the laws of the Congress of the United States, for the more perfect working of the beneficent intentions of the said Order;

And Whereas, With a view to promote this object, and as Grand and Subordinate Lodges of the said Order have been formed or organized in various States and Territories, and will be hereafter formed in various other States and Territories of the United States as well as foreign countries:

1. *Now, therefore, be it known,* that in accordance with the Act of Congress entitled "An Act to provide for the Creation of Corporations in the District of Columbia by General Law," approved May 5, 1870, the undersigned, having associated themselves for the purpose and with the design of establishing and creating the corporation to be known and named the Supreme Lodge of Knights of Pythias, do hereby make and authorize to be filed in the office of the Register of Deeds, in the District of Columbia, this certificate and these articles of association for the government of themselves, their associates, assigns and successors.

2. *And be it further known,* that the beneficial association of which this is the certificate shall be known as the Supreme Lodge of Knights of Pythias, the seal of which has been copyrighted by the Supreme Recording and Corresponding Scribe in the Clerk's Office of the Supreme Court of the District of Columbia.

3. *And be it further known,* that Joseph T. K. Plant, Past Supreme Chancellor Clarence M. Barton of the District of Columbia, Venerable Supreme Patriarch Wilbur H. Myers of Pennsylvania, Supreme Chancellor Samuel Read of New Jersey, Supreme Vice-Chancellor C. L. Russell of Ohio, Supreme Banker W. A. Porter of Pennsylvania, Supreme Guide John F. Comstock of Connecticut, Supreme Inner Steward H. Clay Lloyd of Kentucky, Supreme Outer Steward George H. Crager of Nebraska, Past Supreme Chancellor Edward Dunn, Past Grand Chancellors Harry Kronheimer, J. R. N. Curtin, Francis Woods, Hugh G. Divine, Joseph S. Martin, of the District of Columbia, together with all Past Grand Chancellors of each and every State, Territory or Jurisdiction now organized or hereafter to be organized under the authority of the Supreme Lodge, shall constitute, from and after the filing of this certificate as aforesaid, "The Supreme Lodge of Knights of Pythias of the World."

4. *And be it further known,* that the Board of Trustees of said Supreme Lodge of Knights of Pythias (who shall be elected annually) shall consist of Joseph T. K. Plant, Clarence M. Barton, Edward Dunn, Jos. S. Martin, Francis Wood, Harry Kronheimer, and Hugh Divine, who shall serve until the election of their successors at the annual

session of the Supreme Lodge in April, 1871, and shall serve without pay.

5. *And be it further known*, that no contract for the disbursement of the moneys of the said Supreme Lodge shall be valid and of effect until ratified by the Board of Finance or Financial Committee.

6. *And be it further known*, that the officers of the said Supreme Lodge Knights of Pythias of the World shall consist of Venerable Supreme Patriarch, Supreme Chancellor, Supreme Vice-Chancellor, Supreme Recording and Corresponding Scribe, Supreme Banker, Supreme Guide, Supreme Inner Steward, Supreme Outer Steward, all of whom shall be elected by ballot, every alternate year, on the first day of the session of said Supreme Lodge, and the said Supreme Recording and Corresponding Scribe and Supreme Banker shall give such security for the faithful performance of their duty as may be ordered by said Supreme Lodge.

7. *And be it further known*, that the said Supreme Lodge shall hold an annual session for the transaction of all business for the benefit and welfare of the Order, and that the Supreme Chancellor may, and on the call of fifteen Past Grand Chancellors, or Past Supreme Chancellors, convene the Supreme Lodge at any time business may demand, and all of said annual sessions shall be held in such city or town as the Supreme Lodge may determine upon at a regular session: *Provided*, all special or called sessions shall be held in the city of Washington, D. C.

8. *And be it further known*, that a representative from a majority of the Grand Lodges working under the jurisdiction of this Supreme Lodge shall constitute a quorum for the transaction of business.

9. *And be it further known*, that the said Supreme Lodge shall have power to alter and amend its Constitution and By-Laws, at will, and that it shall have power to prescribe modes of initiation, etc., for the working of said Order; and no Grand or Subordinate Lodges purporting to be Knights of Pythias shall have legal standing unless chartered by or through the regularly elected officers of this Supreme Lodge in regular or called sessions, or by the Supreme Chancellor during the recess of said Supreme Lodge.

In witness whereof we, the undersigned officers and

members of the Supreme Lodge of Knights of Pythias of the World have hereunto affixed our names and seals this —— day of August, A.D. 1870.

Jos. T. K. Plant.	[SEAL]
Edward Dunn.	[SEAL]
Francis Wood.	[SEAL]
Jos. S. Martin.	[SEAL]
Clarence M. Barton.	[SEAL]
H. Kronheimer.	[SEAL]
Hugh G. Divine.	[SEAL]

District of Columbia, } ss.
   County of Washington, }

I, R. H. Marsh, a justice of the peace in and for said county and district, do hereby certify that Jos. T. K. Plant, Clarence M. Barton, Edward Dunn, H. Kronheimer, Francis Wood, Hugh G. Divine, Jos. S. Martin, personally appeared before me in said district and acknowledged the signing of the same to be their voluntary act for the purposes therein set forth.

{ SEAL } Witness my hand and seal this 5th day of August, 1870. R. H. MARSH, J. P.

Indorsements on the filing of the foregoing document:

19   2 00

Incorporation Certificate of the " Supreme Lodge of K. of P.'s Association, D. C."

12

Received for Record, August 5, 1870, and recorded in Liber " Deeds of Incorporation," folio 75, D. C. Ex'd by
54   C. Wolf, Recorder.
(*Jour. 1871, 261, 382; 1874, 848, 849.*)

Amended Act of Incorporation of the Supreme Lodge Knights of Pythias.

156. Whereas, On the fifth day of August, A.D. 1870, it was deemed necessary to incorporate the Supreme Lodge Knights of Pythias of the World, under the act of Congress, approved May 5, A.D. 1870, entitled " An Act to provide for the Creation of Corporations in the District of Columbia, by General Law," and

Whereas, The body corporate thereby created has powers conferred upon them by said law to make proper laws to govern themselves and to alter and amend their act or deed of incorporation; it is therefore, in view of the said law, that the following amendments to said deed of incorporation are acknowledged by the proper officers and members, and placed on file in said district. And it is hereby agreed and understood that everything in these articles different to those in the old articles shall be the act of incorporation, jointly, with so much of the old act as may not be altered by these articles; and which said articles of incorporation are hereby amended and altered as follows:

1. To section two, add the words " and has also been recorded in the office of the Librarian of Congress in the Capitol of the United States at Washington, D. C."

2. That all of section three (3) in the paper filed August 5, 1870, is hereby declared void, and the following is inserted in lieu thereof: " The Supreme Lodge shall consist of all Past Supreme Chancellors; the Supreme Officers and two Representatives from each Grand Lodge under the jurisdiction of said Supreme Lodge until there are 20,000 members under the jurisdiction of a Grand Lodge, and one Supreme Representative for each additional 10,000 members: *Provided*, that no Grand Lodge shall be entitled to more than four (4) Supreme Representatives."

3. That section four (4) be altered to read as follows: " The Board of Trustees shall consist of Supreme Chancellor S. S. Davis, of New Hampshire; S. K. of R. and S. Joseph Dowdall, of Ohio; S. M. of E. John B. Stumph, of Indiana, and Supreme Vice Chancellor D. B. Woodruff, of Georgia, who shall serve until the election of their successors, it being understood that the four principal officers of the Supreme Lodge shall compose the Board of Trustees."

4. That all of section five (5) is hereby annulled.

5. That section six (6) shall hereafter be section five (5) except the words " on the first day of the session of said Supreme Lodge."

6. That section seven (7) shall hereafter be section six (6) and shall read and be as follows: " That the said Supreme Lodge shall hold an annual session at such time and place as a majority of its members present may determine, for the transaction of all business for the benefit and welfare of the Order, and that the Supreme Chancellor may, and on the call of the Supreme Representatives of ten Grand Juris-

dictions in writing, shall convene an extra session of said Supreme Lodge at Washington City, D. C."

7. And further, all succeeding sections are hereby altered in number to correspond as above, and the names of all Supreme Officers are hereby made to agree with the Constitution of the Order. And it is hereby declared that all and singular the parts of the incorporation of August 5, 1870, not altered by this supplementary paper, are hereby ratified and re-affirmed, and that said Supreme Lodge shall be and remain a body corporate for the term of twenty years. And for the purpose of a compliance with the act of Congress heretofore cited we, S. S. Davis, of New Hampshire; Joseph Dowdall, of Ohio; John B. Stumph, of Indiana; and D. B. Woodruff, of Georgia, Officers and Trustees of said Supreme Lodge, Past Supreme Chancellor Jos. T. K. Plant, of the District of Columbia; Past Supreme Chancellor Samuel Read, of New Jersey, and Past Grand Chancellor Frederick D. Stuart, G. J. L. Foxwell, Richard Goodhart, A. T. Cavis, and A. J. Gunning, all of the District of Columbia, as incorporators, have hereunto affixed their hands and seals this fifth day of October, A.D. 1875.

S. S. Davis, S. C.	[SEAL]
Joseph Dowdall, S. K. of R. & S.	[SEAL]
John B. Stumph, S. M. of E.	[SEAL]
D. B. Woodruff, S. V. C.	[SEAL]
Samuel Read, P. S. C.	[SEAL]
Jos. T. K. Plant, P. S. C.	[SEAL]
Fred. D. Stuart, P. G. C.	[SEAL]
G. J. L. Foxwell, P. G. C.	[SEAL]
Richard Goodhart, P. G. C.	[SEAL]
A. T. Cavis, P. G. C.	[SEAL]
A. J. Gunning, P. G. C.	[SEAL]

(*Jour. 1876, 1201, 1202; approved*, id. *1293*.)

(2) Incorporation of Grand and Subordinate Lodges.

157. **Since a Grand Lodge** exists only and solely by and through a charter issued by the Supreme Lodge, the act and articles of incorporation of any Grand or Subordinate Lodge of the Order have no bearing, weight, influence or relation, save as relates to such matters as exist, or may

4

exist, between them and extraneous individuals or corporations. (*Jour. 1874, 934.*)

158. Bodies under control of the Supreme Lodge are prohibited from becoming incorporated under State laws. For the purpose of holding realty, "a committee" or a "Board of Trustees" may become incorporated, but the body should be left out. Grand Bodies already incorporated are required to change the incorporation to a proper "Board." (*Jour. 1874, 867, 868, 928.*)

INSTALLATION.

1. When to take place.
2. Who to install.
3. By proxy.
4. New installation work.
5. Old installation work.

[See Election.]

(1) WHEN TO TAKE PLACE.

159. Officers of a Subordinate Lodge shall be installed at the first regular meeting in the new term, if unforeseen circumstances do not prevent; but no officer shall be installed unless he has fully paid to his Lodge the amount of all dues and claims of whatsoever nature then accrued. [Obligatory.] (*Const., Art. viii, Sec. 2.*)

(2) WHO TO INSTALL.

[See Deputy Supreme Chancellor (in Supreme Lodge); Grand Lodge.]

160. On the appeal of P. C. J. H. K. from the action of the Grand Lodge of Nebraska, the case was this: At the annual session of the Grand Lodge in January, 1872, the Grand Chancellor was absent, and the Vice-Grand Chancellor presided. After an election for officers, the Vice-Grand Chancellor (who had been elected Grand Chancellor) called upon a Past Grand Chancellor to install. Objection was made that by the Ritual of the Order it is provided, "the installation will be performed by the Supreme Chancellor or retiring Grand Chancellor assisted," etc. On motion, a Past Grand Chancellor was requested by the Grand Lodge to install the officers, and the Grand Recording and Corresponding Scribe was instructed to write to the Supreme Chancellor and ask his approval. The installation was then proceeded with. The point made was, that by the Ritual only the Supreme Chancellor or the retiring Grand Chancellor can install the newly elected Grand Officers, and make the official proclamation of their installation. *Held*, that this interpretation was not correct, since, in the absence of the Supreme Chancellor, it would put it in the power of a Grand Chancellor, by remaining away, to prevent the installation of his successor, or, in the event of his death or removal, leave the Grand Lodge dependent upon a visit from the Supreme Chancellor, often a matter of inconvenience, if not of impossibility; and that if neither the Supreme Chancellor or Grand Chancellor be present, it is perfectly regular to have the ceremony performed by a Past Grand Chancellor. (*Jour. 1872, 626.*)

(3) By Proxy.

161. It is contrary to the established customs and ritualistic ceremonies of the Order that, in the absence of an elective Grand Officer at the time of installation, he may be installed by proxy. (*Jour. 1875, 1139.*)

(4) New Installation Work.

162. In 1874 the following resolutions were adopted by the Supreme Lodge with reference to the new installation work:

"*Resolved*, That the Supreme Chancellor and Supreme Keeper of Records and Seal be and they are hereby authorized and ordered to have a sufficient quantity of form for public and private installation and institution of Lodges of this Order, with its accompanying diagrams, plates, notes, references, changes in and form of work printed, to supply the place of the form of 'Installation' now in use by all Subordinate Lodges K. of P., as hereinbefore mentioned and set forth; as also sufficient for any increase of Lodges that may occur prior to the next session of this Supreme Body; and be it further

"*Resolved*, That the Supreme Chancellor and Supreme Keeper of Records and Seal of this Supreme Lodge of the World shall furnish said new and adopted form, through the different Grand Lodges and their proper officers, to said

Subordinate Lodges in whose Grand Jurisdiction they may
be situate, and to all Subordinate Lodges now held under
the special jurisdiction of this Supreme Lodge, at a *minimum*
rate of 30 cents per copy, or $1.50 per set, which *shall* con-
sist of *five*, and in exchange for those of the form now in
use, copy for copy or set for set; or in absence of book for
book *when* exchanging, *full* price, as hereinafter set forth,
must be exacted and paid, after this present form as adopted
is issued and officially promulgated; and thereafter, when
furnished to new or other Lodges as supplies, as follows,
to wit:

" *To Grand Lodges.*— Installation books for Subordinate
Lodges *each* 40 cents, or $2 per set of *five*.

" *To Subordinate Lodges.*—Installation book 60 cents *each*,
or $3 per set of *five;* and be it further

"*Resolved*, That, on and after the 1st day of July, A. D.
1874, and of P. P. the XI, or as soon thereafter as is possible,
that all of the present form of Ritual of Installation now in
use shall be called in by the Supreme Keeper of Records
and Seal, through the proper Grand Officers of the various
Grand Jurisdictions, or Deputy Grand Chancellors, and be
replaced, in the same sources through them, by the form
adopted; and which called in Installation, or those of *that*
form which may be on hand, shall be destroyed by the
Supreme Chancellor and Supreme Keeper of Records and
Seal, or other properly delegated authority by them, within
thirty days thereafter; and be it further

"*Resolved*, That after thirty days from the date of official
issuance and promulgation, the use of the said form of Installation *shall be obligatory*, and the use of the present or
old form now out become illegal in its use, under the pains
and penalties of the law as made and provided by the Grand
Lodges in whose various jurisdictions Lodges may be situate, or of this Supreme Lodge K. of P. of the World; and
be it further

"*Resolved*, That otherwise than as herein expressed the
legislation of this Supreme Lodge, whether constitutional
or otherwise, be and the same is hereby continued in force,
but all other matters pertaining to or in conflict herewith
be and the same is hereby repealed; and be it finally

"*Resolved*, That from and after the issue of the adopted
form of Ceremonial and appendant Work for the use of Sub-

ordinate Lodges of the Order of K. of P., no alteration, amendment, or other changes shall be made in the same (except to make the same comply with the legislation had at this session of the Supreme Lodge, so far as a change in the titles of the officers of Grand Lodges is concerned) for the space of five years, or until the regular session of A.D. 1879 and of P. P. the 16th." (*Jour. 1874, 968, 969.*)

(5) OLD INSTALLATION WORK

163. The use of the *old* installation work is not lawful. (*Jour. 1875, 1158.*)

164. At the session of 1872 the amended O. B. N. was stricken from the installation ceremony, except as to the office of Chancellor Commander. (*Jour. 1872, 534, 599.*)

INSURANCE.

165. "Relief funds," secured by the "insurance feature, are not recognized in nor warranted by clause 22, Sec. 2, Art. VIII of the Supreme Lodge Constitution. (*Jour. 1876, 1288, 1293, 1301.*)

The question in the case referred to on page 1288 arose with reference to the "Constitution of the Minnesota K. of P. Widows and Orphans' Relief Fund," presented to the Supreme Lodge for approval. as an amendment of the Constitution of the Grand Lodge of Minnesota, and which was not approved. See, also, page 1301, where the question arose as to Mortuary Benefit Laws of Illinois.

166. It is illegal to provide, by general compulsory assessment on all the members of the Order in a Grand Jurisdiction, for an "insurance," "relief" or "mortuary fund," in the nature of an insurance on lives. (*Jour. 1876, 1288, 1293, 1301.*)

JEWELS.
[See Uniform, Regalia, etc.]

JOURNAL OF PROCEEDINGS, AND MINUTES.
[See Supreme Keeper of Records and Seal (in Supreme Lodge); Reports.]

167. It shall be obligatory on all Grand and Subordinate Lodges of this Order to have a full volume of Supreme Lodge Proceedings and Laws, as issued, on hand for ready reference on law or usage points; and hereafter for any and all new Subordinate Lodges, one full copy or set of Supreme Lodge Proceedings shall constitute an indispensable part of their supplies to be sent out and paid for. All "sets" of Work, etc., as herein enumerated, shall constitute the legal number to be issued by any and all Grand Lodges or Officers, which shall neither be added to nor taken from by them; and all work delivered to Grand and Subordinate Lodges or Officers ordering the same must be paid for on date of delivery, free of expense to the Supreme Lodge. (*Const., Art. xxvii.*)

[See, also, Jour. 1869, 107; 1875, 1154.]

168. In 1873 directions were given by the Supreme Lodge as to the method of printing the Journals, that there be a difference in the type used on that portion which contains the action of the body, so that it may stand out more distinctly from the subjects upon which they pass, and be thereby more available as a work of reference. (*Jour. 1873, 741.*)

169. At the session of 1875 the Supreme K. of R. and S. was authorized to contract for all the printing connected with his office, including the Journal of 1875; and also all work necessary to obtain an edition of the Journal from the organization to and including the session of 1874, and have the same bound in law binding, provided the rates of cost were not more than the work of the same kind done in 1874. Owing, however, to the small number of orders therefor, the undertaking of replacing the destroyed stereotype plates of the Proceedings prior to 1871 was abandoned.

[See Jour. 1873, 741; 1874, 936; 1875, 1113, 1154; 1876, 1245.]

170. All Grand Lodges are required to forward to the office of the Supreme K. of R. and S. two complete sets of their Journals of Proceedings, and each year, or so soon thereafter as printed, two copies of the same.

The Supreme K. of R. and S. is required to have the same bound in suitable sized volumes in legal style, one set to be retained in the office of the Supreme K. of R. and S., the other to be retained in the office of the Supreme Chancellor. This resolution to go into effect as soon as 'he funds of the Supreme Lodge will permit.

Grand Lodges are requested to have their Journals of

Proceedings uniform in size with the Proceedings of the Supreme Lodge. (*Jour. 1875, 1124.*)

171. The resolution adopted at the adjourned session of the Supreme Lodge, in Wilmington, Delaware, November 10, 1868, requiring German Lodges to render their Proceedings in the English language, is rescinded. (*Jour. 1870, 221.*)

LAWS, LEGISLATION, Etc.

1. When in force.
2. Obligatory.
3. Hypothetical cases.
4. Amendments.
5. Resolutions, etc., to be presented in writing.

[See, also, Supreme Lodge ; Committees ; Constitutions ; Sessions.]

(1) When in Force.

172. All laws, enactments, or legislation of the Supreme Lodge becomes of force from date of passage and publication. (*Const., Art. xiv.*)

[See Jour. 1872, 620.]

(2) Obligatory.

173. The legislative acts of the Supreme Lodge, when they accord with the Supreme Lodge Constitution, are binding and obligatory upon Grand and Subordinate Lodges and members. (*Jour. 1876, 1232, 1302.*)

174. A decision of a Supreme Chancellor stands as law until repealed. (*Jour. 1875, 1034, 1045; Const., Art. iii, Sec. 2.*)

(3) Hypothetical Cases.

175. Neither the Supreme Chancellor nor the Supreme Lodge will hereafter receive or answer any hypothetical propositions or questions submitted to them either in recess or during the session of the Supreme Lodge, except the same come from a Grand Lodge or a Subordinate Lodge under the jurisdiction of this Supreme Lodge, and under the seal thereof. (*Jour. 1876, 1311.*)

(4) Amendments.

176. Any member of the Supreme Lodge has the privilege of submitting amendments of the Supreme Lodge laws to the Committee on Laws and Supervision for their consideration. (*Jour. 1870, 223.*)

(5) RESOLUTIONS, ETC., TO BE PRESENTED IN WRITING.

177. All resolutions and motions of length presented to the Supreme Lodge are required to be written upon half-sheet letter paper, in legible handwriting, folded twice, and properly backed, with a title referring to the subject-matter contained therein, and the signature of the member offering the same. (*Jour. 1870, 224.*)

LOTTERIES, GIFT ENTERPRISES, ETC.

178. No Grand Lodge, nor Subordinate Lodge of this Order, nor any individual member of any Lodge, shall, in the name of the Order, resort to, institute or promote any scheme of raffle, lotteries, gift enterprises, or schemes of chance of any kind. Any Grand Lodge violating this rule shall forfeit its charter to the Supreme Lodge. Any Subordinate Lodge violating this rule shall forfeit its charter to its Grand Lodge. Any individual member of any Lodge who shall violate this rule shall be suspended from the Order. (*Jour. 1876, 1232, 1264, 1299.*)

MEMBERSHIP.

1. Applications for initiation.
2. Applications for affiliation.
3. Solicitation of candidates.
4. Effect of rejection or protest.
5. Fees.
6. Qualifications for membership.
7. Residence.

[See Subordinate Lodges.]

(1) APPLICATIONS FOR INITIATION.

179. Applications for initiation must be signed by the petitioner, stating his age, residence and occupation, and indorsed by two Knights in good standing, who are members of the Lodge, which must be entered on the records, and the petition referred to a committee of three for investigation (neither of whom shall have recommended him), whose duty it shall be to report on the character and qualifications of the petitioner at a regular meeting. The applicant shall then be balloted for by secret ball ballot, and, if approved, he may be admitted. [Obligatory.] (*Const., Art. viii, Sec. 2.*)

180. No proposition for membership shall be withdrawn, unless by consent of the Lodge, after it has been referred to a committee; and all cases so referred shall be balloted for upon the report of the committee, whether it be favorable or unfavorable. [Obligatory.] (*Const., Art. viii, Sec. 2.*)

Prior to the adoption of the new Constitution it was held that an application for membership could not be withdrawn by unanimous consent after report of committee was read. A petition once submitted, read to the Lodge, referred to a committee, and reported upon by said committee, became Lodge property, could not be withdrawn under any circumstances, but must go to ballot and take its chances. (*Jour. 1873, App. 38.*)

181. An applicant for membership who, having been elected for the Page rank, and before being instructed in it, is found to be unworthy, from facts not made known when his case was before the Lodge, may be refused admission by a majority vote of the Lodge present; and if rejected the fee must be returned to him. While this principle should be general, it is, under the present Constitution, a proper subject for local legislation, and the above rule is therefore obligatory only upon Lodges under the immediate jurisdiction of the Supreme Lodge. (*Jour. 1875, 1114.*)

(2) APPLICATIONS FOR AFFILIATION.

182. Any brother of the Order, in good standing, desirous of becoming a member of a Lodge, shall make application as in the case of an uninitiated person, and accompany same with his withdrawal card from the Lodge of which he was last a member, or the card granted by the Grand Lodge in lieu thereof, which shall be referred to a committee of three, whose duty it shall be to report as to the standing and qualifications of the applicant at a regular meeting. The brother shall then be balloted for by secret ball ballot, as in the case of an initiate. [Obligatory.] (*Const., Art. viii, Sec. 2.*)

(3) SOLICITATION OF CANDIDATES.

183. Great caution and discrimination should be exercised in the matter of soliciting candidates for membership in the Order. (*Jour. 1871, 401, 413.*)

184. At a subsequent date the Supreme Chancellor, on the authority of the preceding section, ruled that members of the Order are not permitted to solicit citizens to join. (*Jour. 1873, App. 39.*)

(4) EFFECT OF REJECTION OR PROTEST.

185. A brother holding a withdrawal card in force, who applies to a Lodge for membership by said card, and is rejected, may apply to any other Lodge, or in the absence of any local law, to the same Lodge at any time. The relations and privileges of a member of the Order are entirely different from an applicant for initiation. The former has some rights in the Order, the latter none. (*Jour. 1876, 1228, 1296.*)

186. Rejected material cannot be accepted by the Deputy Grand Chancellor on a roll of charter members for a new Lodge, where such fact is existing and known to him; if done innocently or negligently it is censurable, but not criminal; further, it ought always be made a preliminary interrogatory, "Have you ever applied to any Lodge of this Order and been rejected?" If the answer is negative, then proceed; if afterward found to be a falsehood, the penal law should be applied in its most stringent shape. (*Jour. 1873, App. 39.*)

187. One Lodge of the Knights of Pythias cannot accept of rejected material from another Lodge in the same locality, even after the expiration of the six months' probation required by the Lodge to which the first application was made, without the consent of the Lodge rejecting in the first place. This is another matter wholly local in character, but so long as under the control of the Supreme Lodge, they cannot. (*Jour. 1873, App. 39.*)

188. The Deputy Grand Chancellor cannot proceed to initiate the charter members of a new Lodge, upon the receipt of a dispensation, over the protest of another Lodge already in existence. The protest or objection being filed in regular form, and on valid grounds, must be heard and passed upon, and orders issued from the office of the Supreme Chancellor to proceed before it can be done. (*Jour. 1873, App. 39.*)

The legislation as appearing in the three preceding paragraphs refers only to Lodges under the immediate jurisdiction of the Supreme Lodge, being in answer to queries from the Hawaiian Islands.

(5) FEES.

189. Every application for membership must be accompanied with the initiation fee, the amount of which shall be fixed by each Grand Lodge; *Provided*, That in no case shall the three ranks be conferred in North America for a less amount than ten dollars; *Provided, further*, That the Supreme Chancellor be and he is hereby authorized and empowered, upon the application of a Grand Lodge, through its proper officers, to issue his dispensation authorizing and permitting such jurisdiction to confer the three ranks of the Order for a sum not less than six dollars. [Obligatory.] (*Const., Art. viii, Sec. 2.*)

190. The provision fixing a minimum as to fees for conferring the ranks is obligatory, and cannot be changed, except as provided in Art. XXXII. While the minimum should be fixed by the Supreme Lodge, below which no Lodge should be permitted to confer the ranks, yet, with that restriction, the question as to the amount of fees for conferring rank, subject to the restriction before stated, of right ought to be left in the hands of the several Grand Jurisdictions. (*Jour. 1876, 1286.*)

191. No rank shall be conferred under any pretense whatever, unless the same shall have been previously paid for. [Obligatory.] (*Const., Art. viii, Sec. 2.*)

192. There is no constitutional authority for opening "charter books" so called, so that a Lodge may receive members or applications for a less sum than fixed by the Constitution; and a dispensation for that purpose cannot be issued. (*Jour. 1875, 1033, 1113.*)

193. A Grand Chancellor cannot grant dispensations to initiate persons for less than the rates prescribed by law, even though he have directions and authority from his Grand Lodge so to do. (*Jour. 1873, 768.*)

194. The refunding or donating, or promising directly or indirectly to refund or donate, to applicants for membership in this Order, any portion of the initiation fee, is a violation of Art. VIII, Sec. 8, of the Constitution. (*Jour. 1875, 1133, 1140.*)

(6) QUALIFICATIONS FOR MEMBERSHIP.

195. No person shall be initiated into a Subordinate Lodge of this Order who has not reached the legal age or majority in the country where the Lodge is located, nor unless he be a white male, of good moral character, sound in health, and a believer in a Supreme Being. [Obligatory.] (*Const., Art. viii, Sec. 2.*)

[See, also, Jour. 1873, App. 15.]

196. The following query was offered by Supreme Representative Woodruff, of Georgia: "Has a Subordinate Lodge the right to reject an applicant between the age of twenty-one and fifty, the age being the only objection? Or, in other words, can a Subordinate Lodge frame its By-Laws prescribing the age of twenty-one as the minimum and the age of forty as the maximum?" The subject was referred to the Committee on Laws and Supervision, who reported on the document that "The committee recommend its adoption." (*Jour. 1872, 591, 611.*)

Query, What did they adopt?

197. Persons who are physically or mentally unable to comply with the "Ritual and Work" are improper persons to be initiated Knights of Pythias. (*Jour. 1872, 472.*)

198. Persons who cannot write are ineligible for membership in the Order. (*Jour. 1870, 204, 229 ; 1873, App. 35.*)

199. If a candidate can write his name he is entitled to advance. (*Jour. 1873, 768.*)

200. Every person initiated must be twenty-one years of age; nor can the Supreme Chancellor dispense with this requirement. (*Jour. 1869, 68, 101.*)

[See Jour. 1868, 45, 47.]

201. The Constitution of the Order does not permit

the initiation of natives of the Hawaiian Islands and their descendants. (*Jour. 1875, 1129.*)

202. The Supreme Lodge does not recognize Lodges of the Order composed of ladies, persons under age, or colored persons; and the Supreme Chancellor is authorized to make such public declaration or publication of this fact as may in his judgment be necessary to prevent deception or imposition. (*Jour. 1871, 382.*)

203. Lodges composed of colored persons cannot be formed under the jurisdiction of the Supreme Lodge, nor can colored persons be admitted as members in any Subordinate Lodge of this Order. (*Jour. 1871, 379, 383.*)

204. Although the rule of law is that candidates for initiation in Subordinate Lodges must be perfect in all their limbs, yet it is competent for the Supreme Lodge to dispense with this requirement in individual cases. (*Jour.1870, 210.*)

[See Jour. 1870, 202 ; 1873, App. 35.]

205. The discretion in regard to the initiation of maimed persons, which, by resolution at top of page 745, Journal of 1873, is allowed to Grand Lodges when in session, is now extended to Grand Chancellors during the recess. (*Jour. 1876, 1285, 1294.*)

The resolution itself, which is as follows —

"*Resolved*, That the laws of this Order do not require the suspension of a member who, after his initiation, has been maimed.

"*Resolved*, That this Supreme Lodge hereby authorize any Grand Lodge, in open session, to grant a dispensation to any of its Subordinates to initiate a maimed person into the Order: *Provided*, that in no instance shall a dispensation be granted to a person incapable of making an honest livelihood for himself and family"—

does not appear from the Journal to have been acted upon, till it was adopted (at least the last one) by reference in 1876, in the terms above stated.

206. In 1874 the Supreme Chancellor decided that applications coming from Subordinate Lodges under the immediate jurisdiction of the Supreme Lodge, for dispensations to admit maimed persons, must be made to the Supreme Chancellor by vote, and under the seal of the Subordinate Lodge, approved by the Deputy Supreme Chancellor of the jurisdiction; and that the Supreme Chancellor might grant a dispensation for the admission of a maimed person, if in his judgment it appears proper, subject to the same restrictions made to Grand Lodges, viz.: the applicant must be capable of earning a livelihood for himself and family. (*Jour. 1875, 1040.*)

This decision was approved by the Supreme Lodge, who enacted that thereafter dispensations might be granted by the Supreme Chancellor to admit maimed persons in Lodges under the jurisdiction of the Supreme Lodge, in pursuance of regulations adopted by the then Supreme Chancellor, and subject to the restrictions theretofore prescribed for cases of maimed persons. (*Jour. 1875, 1114.*)

(7) RESIDENCE.

207. No rank shall be conferred on a brother who is a non-resident of the jurisdiction, or who is a member of another Lodge, without first obtaining the permission of the Lodge to which the brother is attached. [Obligatory.] (*Const., Art. viii, Sec. 2.*)

208. A candidate for membership, residing in a jurisdiction other than the one in which his proposition is offered, shall not be initiated without the written consent of the Lodge nearest his residence. [Obligatory.] (*Const., Art. viii, Sec. 2.*)

[See, also, Jour. 1872, 580; 1873, App. 37.]

209. Where a Lodge in Massachusetts received applications for membership from persons residing in the jurisdiction of New Hampshire, in a city where a Lodge existed, and initiated them after being informed that they were not residents of Massachusetts, and with a protest in their hands against such act, whereupon charges were preferred against such Lodge, and the Lodge suspended, the Grand Lodge on appeal providing for reinstituting said Lodge when a number of the former members, who were in no way implicated in the irregularities complained of, should make application to the Grand Officers, and declaring that no one implicated in the cause of this complaint, with such as were received out of the jurisdiction of Massachusetts, should ever be received into membership, by which action of the Grand Lodge none but the guilty were made to suffer: *Held*, on appeal to the Supreme Lodge, that the action of the Grand Lodge was legal, and should be sustained. (*Jour. 1872, 538, 573.*)

MILEAGE AND PER DIEM.
[See, also, Committee.]

210. **The Supreme Lodge** shall pay the mileage and necessary expenses of its officers and representatives to and while in Supreme Session, unless otherwise provided for. The mileage shall be at the rate of four cents per mile, and four dollars per day during the actual session of the body. (*Const., Art. 11.*)

211. **No Supreme Lodge Officer** or Grand Representative is entitled to receive mileage and expenses unless he is present at the close of the session, or is excused by the Supreme Chancellor. (*Jour. 1869, 94.*)

212. **No Supreme Lodge Representative,** elected to office therein, shall receive mileage, etc., for both offices. (*Jour. 1870, 221.*)

MINUTES.
[See Journal of Proceedings.]

NOMINATIONS.
[See Elections.]

213. **Nominations** for the elective officers of a Subordinate Lodge may be made on the night preceding and on the night of election. (*Const., Art. viii, Sec. 2, clause 5.*)

214. **Sec. 2,** (clause 5) Art. VIII, of the Supreme Lodge Constitution authorizes independent nominations on the night of election, and not merely the confirmation of those previously made. (*Jour. 1875, 1140.*)

A number of decisions have been made under the old Constitution respecting nominations, which are here presented:

On the appeal of P. G. C. H. C. L. from the decision of the Grand Lodge of Kentucky, in the matter of Mystic Lodge, No. 11, the facts were as follows:

A Vice Chancellor, desiring to be absent, tendered his resignation, in lieu of which the Lodge allowed him leave of absence. Upon his failing to report at the proper time, or to send any excuse, the resignation was accepted, thereby creating a vacancy. The W. C. then announced nominations in order, when the point was raised whether it would be in order to nominate, elect and install upon that same night. The W. C. ruled that it would not be in order, but that nominations must be made in advance of the night of election. Upon appeal to the Lodge his ruling was sustained. An appeal was taken to the Grand Lodge, when the decision of the Lodge was reversed. The law relied on was the Constitution of Mystic Lodge, wherein it says " that vacancies occurring by reason of death, resignation or otherwise shall be filled in the manner of the original selection. *Held*, that the matter was fully decided in the [old] Constitution recommended for the adoption of Subordinate Lodges, in Sec. 4, Art. II, which was obligatory upon them, providing that " Nominations for all the above elective officers shall be made on the night preceding and on the night of election, except to fill a vacancy," which is susceptible of but one interpretation, to wit : that in all elections to fill a vacancy nominations may be made upon the night of election.

The words " original selection," contained in Sec. 6 of the same article, can only be construed to refer to the manner of voting, to wit : by ballot, in order that one section of this article may not contradict the other. (*Jour. 1872, 566, 625.*)

On appeal of H. C. B., Grand R. and C. S., Grand Lodge K. of P. of Illinois, contesting a credential issued to P. G. C. J. J. H., the facts were briefly these :

At the semi-annual session held July 17, 1871, of the Grand Lodge of Illinois, the Grand Chancellor, in his address referring to the subject of Emeritus P. G. C., which was before the Supreme Body at its session in 1871 from that jurisdiction, stated the action of the Supreme Lodge, declaring past elections null and void, and recommended that all candidates there to be nominated for such honor should be from Lodges represented at the July term, 1870. The Committee on Address recommended the adoption of this suggestion; their report was adopted, and the minutes of that session were confirmed at the next, thus fully ratifying the suggestion of the Grand Chancellor. Among the nominations was that of P. C. H., who at that time was a member of Lodge No. 6, and came within the rule. At the January session, 1872, when the election was to be had, (H. having in the meantime withdrawn from No. 6, and been instrumental in organizing a new Lodge, No. 21, which had not been represented in July, 1870, to which he then belonged,) the Grand Chancellor ruled his nomination irregular. Upon this ruling being announced a motion was made and carried, " That it is the sense of this Grand Lodge that Rep. J. J. H., No. 21, be recognized as a candidate for P. G. C. in the present election about to transpire." Some discussion took place, but afterward the Grand Lodge proceeded to an election, when Rep. H. was elected by a large vote.

The appeal was taken upon wholly technical grounds, on account of irregularities in the election. *Held*, that although the irregularities complained of were such as should have been rectified at the time, still they were fully cured by the vote of the Grand Lodge upon the motion above recited, and were confirmed by the subsequent election of H., and that this action should not now be disturbed. (*Jour. 1872, 574, 447.*)

Under Art. V, Sec. 2, [old] Grand Lodge Constitution, nominations, duly and lawfully made at the July session, cannot be opened, unless all the candidates for office or officers have declined, or removed from the State. (*Jour. 1870, 199.*)

A Grand Lodge has ample power to dispose of the question as to whether nominations for Grand Lodge Officers shall be made in January instead of July. (*Jour. 1870, 200.*)

All Grand Lodges holding annual sessions only are authorized to nominate officers for election at each annual session. (*Jour. 1870, 219.*)

O. B. N.
[See Higher Degrees ; Installation.]

OFFENSES AND THEIR PUNISHMENT.

1. Suspension of Grand Lodges.
2. Method of proceeding upon charges in Grand Lodges.
3. Suspension of Subordinate Lodges.
4. Status of suspended brothers.
5. Reinstatement.
6. Expulsion.
7. Giving untrue answers to questions at initiation.
8. Using emblems as a means of advertising.
9. Disclosing vote.

[See, also, Supreme Chancellor (in Supreme Lodge); Dues; Membership; Delinquent or Defunct Lodges; Withdrawal Cards.]

(1) SUSPENSION OF GRAND LODGES.
[See Grand Lodges.]

215. **That the Supreme Chancellor,** during a recess of the Supreme Lodge, may, for insubordination and revolt on the part of a Grand Lodge or its officers, in refusing to carry into effect and, by obstructing the enforcement of the legislation of the Supreme Lodge, suspend such Grand Lodge and its officers, and place the Grand Jurisdiction in charge of a D. G. C. till the case is acted upon by the Supreme Lodge, seems settled by the "O. B. N." difficulty in Maryland (*Jour. 1871, 262, 386, 387, 419*) and Pennsylvania (*Jour. 1871, 275, 386, 388, 423, 424, 419*), and the Pennsylvania case in relation to the Revised Ritual (*infra*).

216. **Where the Grand Lodge** of Pennsylvania, through its Grand Officers, refused to carry out the legislation of the Supreme Lodge, adopting a certain Revised Ritual of Ceremonial for the general use of the Order in place of the old Ritual then in use, and, through its Grand Officers, assumed and continued in an attitude of positive contumacy, ending in open actions of defiance to the Supreme enactments, such Grand Officers acting in violation of a resolution of the Grand Lodge adopted (after the commencement of the controversy, but before the said acts of open contumacy of such Grand Officers), accepting such Revised Rit-

5

ual, and disavowing any intended contumacy on the part of
the Grand Lodge to the Supreme Lodge; the acts of contumacy of the Grand Officers consisting of a proclamation
and order prohibiting the Subordinate Lodges from holding
any official communication with the S. C., and S. R. and C.
S., or any other Supreme Lodge Officer, except through
the medium of the Grand Lodge, and prohibiting them
from forwarding the old Rituals directly to the S. R. and
C. S. in exchange for the new (the Supreme Officers having opened up a source of supply of the Revised Rituals
directly to said Subordinate Lodges), and directing that the
S. A. P. W. of the jurisdiction for the past term (the new
one having by reason of their contumacy been denied them)
be continued in use until the one for the current term had
been received; whereupon the Supreme Chancellor suspended and annulled the charter of said Grand Lodge, and
organized the State into a district until reorganized by the
Supreme Law, and placed such district in charge of a D.G.C.,
with directions to carry out the legislation of the Supreme
Lodge, etc.: *Held*, by resolution of the Supreme Lodge,
that the actions of the Supreme Chancellor be confirmed,
and that immediately upon the Grand Lodge of Pennsylvania signifying its willingness to comply with all the requirements of the Supreme Lodge, it be restored to its rights
and privileges as a Grand Jurisdiction (*Jour. 1873, 714,
715; App. 44, et seq.*) Which being done the Grand Lodge
was restored to all its rights and prerogatives as a Grand
Lodge (*id. 719*), and the acts of all Subordinate Lodges, and
the Grand Lodge Officers of the Grand Jurisdiction while
acting and working under the old Ritual, subsequent to the
order of promulgation of the Revised Ritual, were legal-
ized; and all disabilities resulting from the non-conformity
on the part of said Grand Lodge to said order of promulgation were removed from those upon whom the several
grades of rank had been conferred under the old Ritual,
subsequent to the date of operation of said order of promulgation (*id. 769.*)

(2) METHOD OF PROCEEDING UPON CHARGES IN GRAND LODGES.

217. As a general proposition, there are no written
rules or declaratory law for conducting proceedings upon

charges against a Grand Lodge Officer. The right to try, to suspend, even to remove, must, perforce, exist. A Grand Lodge, therefore, during the pendency of charges against the Grand Chancellor, may by resolution lawfully vacate such office and order the Vice-Grand Chancellor to act as Grand Chancellor in the interval. (*Jour. 1875, 1128.*)

218. Where charges were preferred in a Grand Lodge in regular form against a representative and member thereof for publishing in a report to the Grand Lodge a false and malicious libel upon a Subordinate Lodge, which charges the Grand Lodge refused to hear, but declared them "out of order," and upon application therefor the party accused, then acting as Grand Scribe of the State, refused to return the charges to the representative of the Lodge injured, whereupon the Lodge appealed to the Supreme Lodge for a hearing; it was ordered that the papers in the case be referred back to the Grand Lodge, and that the said Grand Lodge be required to give them a fair and proper consideration, and the parties a hearing. (*Jour. 1871, 346, 423.*)

219. Where the General Laws of a Grand Lodge, regulating the procedure upon charges and specifications, in their primary meaning refer only to Subordinate Lodges; yet, while they are not obligatory upon the Grand Lodge as a rule of action for its own government, there is no impropriety in their being used as a guide for the action of the Grand Lodge when called upon to act in an analagous case. (*Jour. 1875, 1128.*)

(3) SUSPENSION OF SUBORDINATE LODGES.
[See Delinquent or Defunct Lodges.]

220. The Supreme and each Grand Lodge may provide for and order the revocation of any or all dispensations or charters and suspension of Subordinate Lodges under their jurisdiction for violations of this Constitution, Supreme Lodge orders, enactments, legislation or decisions, or their Grand Lodge constitutional provisions, local laws, or Grand Chancellors' official mandates during recess. (*Const., Art. xxxi.*)

(4) STATUS OF SUSPENDED BROTHERS.

221. A brother suspended for non-payment of dues

ceases to be a member of the Order until reinstated. (*Jour. 1870, 225.*)

222. **The status** of suspended brothers is a matter for Grand Lodge legislation. (*Jour. 1873, 690, 734.*)

(5) REINSTATEMENT.

223. **The question** whether or not it is lawful for a Subordinate Lodge, with the approval of the Grand Lodge and Grand Chancellor, to prescribe in its By-Laws that a member suspended for other reasons than non-payment of dues, and desiring reinstatement, shall not be admitted except upon application and ballot, the same as application for initiation, and payment of the amount standing against him at the time of suspension; also, that such member so reinstated shall not become beneficial for six months after restoration, presents a matter for local legislation, not proper for determination by the Supreme Lodge. (*Jour. 1876, 1284, 1300.* See, also, *Jour. 1873, 690, 734,* where the doctrine is laid down without limitation, that the mode and manner of reinstatement of suspended brothers is a matter for Grand Lodge legislation.)

224. **The question** of the manner of application for reinstatement, by one suspended for non-payment of dues, and the vote thereon, is a subject for local legislation. (*Jour. 1874, 902, 909.*)

225. **A member suspended** for non-payment of dues, wishing to be reinstated, should pay the amount of one year's dues and all assessments charged during that year. Beyond this, it is discretionary with the Lodge. This decision applies only to Lodges working under the direct control of the Supreme Lodge. (*Jour. 1875, 1043, 1114.*)

226. **On the appeal** of H. C. L. against the action of the Grand Lodge of Kentucky, the facts were these: A member who had been suspended for non-payment of dues, having paid up all his arrearages, claimed that he was thereby reinstated without any written application to the Lodge or further action on his part. His claim was allowed by the Lodge, and upon appeal to the Grand Lodge such action was sustained and the appeal dismissed. An appeal was taken from the decision of the Grand Lodge. The provision of the local law on this subject was as follows, to wit:

"*Provided, however*, a brother suspended for non-payment of dues shall be reinstated by paying up all arrearages." *Held*, that the appeal should be dismissed, and the action of the Grand Lodge was sustained. (*Jour. 1872, 566, 588.*)

The Supreme Lodge, however, declined to make the rule of the case general by the adoption of the following resolution, which was lost by a vote of 44 to 4:

"*Resolved*, That any member who has been suspended for non-payment of dues shall upon payment in full of all arrearages so due by him, be thereby forthwith reinstated into good standing without hindrance or further action on the part of the Lodge, provided he be not under sentence of suspension or expulsion for any other offense." (*Jour. 1872, 589.*)

(6) Expulsion.

227. **No member** can be expelled from the Order, but may be suspended for an indefinite number of years. (*Jour. 1868, 18.*)

(7) Giving Untrue Answers to Questions at Initiation.

[See Membership.]

228. **On an appeal** of J. T. P. *v.* Grand Lodge of New Jersey, it appeared that the plaintiff was suspended for a period of five years by his Lodge, on the grounds of not giving true answers to the questions propounded at the time of initiation, and which finding was approved by the Grand Lodge.

The evidence in this case was of a conflicting character, and the committee being unable to detect any criminal intent on the part of the appellant, the appeal was sustained. (*Jour. 1874, 938.*)

(8) Using Emblems, etc., as a Means of Advertising.

229. **No member** of the Order has the right to make use of the name of the Order publicly in any manner for pecuniary benefit, except in advertising periodicals, supplies, or regalia for the Order. (*Jour. 1870, 229.*)

230. **The display** by members of the Order at their places of business of any of the emblems or insignia of the Order, or the use of the same in any manner as a means of advertising, save by those parties who may be engaged in the manufacture or sale thereof, is highly reprehensible, and where made, the Subordinate Lodges should draw the attention of the offender to the matter, and, if persisted in, proceed against him under the law.   (*Jour. 1875, 1133, 1143.*)

(9) Disclosing Vote.

231. The question whether or not it is lawful for one member of a Lodge to be allowed to disclose to another member of the Lodge or Order the name of a brother who may speak or vote against a candidate for membership, presents a matter for local legislation not proper for determination by the Supreme Lodge.   (*Jour. 1876, 1284, 1300.*)

OFFICIAL MEMORIAL MEMBERSHIP CHART.

232. At its session in 1874 the Supreme Lodge adopted and provided for the issue of an Official Memorial Membership Chart and Patent of the Order; prescribed the design, forms, specifications, regulations, distinctions, colors, arrangement of placing same, etc.; created a permanent committee, consisting of the P. S. C., S. C., S. K. of R. and S., to superintend the issuing of the same and carry its legislation on the subject into effect; and also officially recommended its purchase by every member of the Order. (*Jour. 1874, 980.*)

233. By this legislation the Supreme Lodge also withdrew, rescinded and annulled any and all official recognition theretofore given, any chart issued by individuals or concerns, and requested the different Grand Lodges to *order* their Subordinate Lodges to thereafter only use or attach their seals, either in impress or imprint, to none other than the Official Memorial Chart of the Order, as issued by the Supreme Chancellor. (*Jour. 1874, 980.*)

Any and all revenues arising from the sale of the Official Memorial Charts, after paying all legitimate expenses arising therefrom, or necessary thereto, shall become part of the regular revenue of the Supreme Lodge for all future time to come, subject to such changes as may be deemed necessary from time to time, or until repealed or rescinded by that body when in Supreme Convention assembled. (*Jour. 1874, 980.*)

APPENDANT DETAILS OF MEMORIAL CHART.

Form, Size and Shape.—Same as that of Subordinate Charter. Plate submitted herewith.

Plan.—Use Subordinate Charter Plate stone as it is, except the center, which is to be taken out, and lettering as per following forms, "A," "B," and "C," inserted in its place as per following

SPECIFICATIONS.

Form "A."—For members of the third or chivalric rank of "Knight." Border to be the same as now on Subordinate Charter Plate, in tinted black, and lettering to be "black" or "blue," at option of purchaser, by paying the additional cost for the latter.

Form "B."—For members of the Past Chancellor rank. Same as Form "A" in every particular, except in lettering—to be in "black" or "green," at option of purchaser, by paying the additional cost for the latter.

Form "C."—For members of Past Grand Chancellor rank. Same as in forms "A" and "B" in every particular, except lettering—to be in "black" or "red," at option of purchaser, by paying the additional cost for the latter.

Supreme Lodge Imprint Seal.—To be in "red" on all "*black*" or "*green*" lettered charts, and "purple" or "green" on all "*red*" *colored* lettered charts. (*Jour. 1874, 980.*)

MANNER TO BE SOLD.

No chart or charts to be permitted shipped or sent to any person or place or under any pretext *whatsoever*, except—

First, That post-office orders, bank drafts, or checks payable at sight, that are good on solvent institutions, or money for amount, accompany the order for the number of the charts desired; or,

Second, When ordered sent per express to destination they must go "C. O. D." with return collection, express charges added. (*Jour. 1874, 982.*)

234. **The Official Memorial Chart** and Patent of Membership is now furnished by the Supreme Keeper of Records and Seal to the Grand Keepers of Records and Seal, and through them to the several Subordinate Lodges in the same manner as all other supplies. (*Jour. 1875, 1155.*)

FORM FOR OFFICIAL MEMORIAL CHART "A."

And know ye that

The Supreme Lodge of the World hereby issues this Memorial Chart and general and authentic Patent of the Order, bearing its imprint seal, to Grand and Subordinate Lodges of this chivalric Order, to evidence over a proper official seal that our Knightly Brother has been regularly "initiated" in the *first* or "Page" rank, "proved" in the *second* or armorial rank of "Esquire," and "charged" in the *third* or chivalric rank of "Knight," and enrolled as a member on the — day of ——, A.D. 18—, P.P. ——, of —— Lodge, No. —, of the Grand Jurisdiction of ——.

In testimony whereof we have caused to be affixed the official signatures of the proper officers, attested by the seal of this Lodge.　　　　　　　—— C. C. —— V. C.
　　　　　　　　　　　　　　　　　—— K. of R. and S.

Form "A" to be printed as follows, to wit:

No. 1, all in black and tinted same as charter plate, *lettering in "black."*

No 2, border in black and tinted same as charter plate center, *lettering in "blue."* (*Jour. 1874, 982.*)

FORM FOR OFFICIAL MEMORIAL CHART "B."

And know ye that

The Supreme Lodge of the World hereby issues this Memorial Chart and general and authentic Patent of the Order, bearing its imprint seal, to Grand and Subordinate Lodges of this chivalric Order, to evidence over a proper official seal that our Knightly Brother has been regularly "initiated" in the *first* or "Page" rank, "proved" in the *second* or armorial rank of "Esquire," and "charged" in the *third* or chivalric rank of "Knight," and enrolled as a member on the — day of ——, A.D. 18—, P.P. —, of —— Lodge, No. —, and thereafter admitted and instructed as of the high, honorable and Past-official rank of "PAST CHANCELLOR," and his name blazoned as such on the Grand Roster of Gold of the Grand Lodge of the Grand Jurisdiction of ——.

In testimony whereof we have caused to be affixed the official signatures of the proper officers, attested by the seal of this Lodge.　　　　　　　—— C. C. —— V. C.
　　　　　　　　　　　　　　　　　—— K. of R. and S.

Form "B" to be printed as follows, to wit:

No. 1, all in black and tinted same as charter plate, *letter-ing in "black."*

No. 2, border in black and tinted same as charter plate center, *lettering in "green."* (*Jour. 1874, 982.*)

FORM FOR OFFICIAL MEMORIAL CHART "C."

And know ye that

The Supreme Lodge of the World hereby issues this Memorial Chart and general and authentic Patent of the Order, bearing its imprint seal, to Grand and Subordinate Lodges of this chivalric Order, to evidence over a proper official seal that our Knightly Brother has been regularly "initiated" in the *first* or "Page" rank, "proved" in the *second* or armorial rank of "Esquire," and "charged" in the *third* or chivalric rank of "Knight," and enrolled as a member on the — day of ——, A.D. 18 —, P.P. —, of —— Lodge, No. —, and thereafter admitted and instructed as of the high, honorable and Past-official rank of " PAST CHAN-CELLOR," and his name blazoned as such on the Grand Roster of Gold of the Grand Lodge of the Grand Jurisdiction of ——, as also appearing by proper record of having been in regular form admitted, instructed, and invested with the work and prerogatives of the Supreme rank of "PAST GRAND CHANCELLOR" by the Supreme Lodge of the World.

In testimony whereof we have caused to be affixed the official signatures of the proper officers, attested by the seal of this Lodge. —— C. C. —— V. C.

—— K. of R. and S.

Form "C" to be printed as follows, to wit:

No. 1, all in black and tinted same as charter plate, *letter-ing in "black."*

No. 2, border in black and tinted same as charter plate center, *lettering in "red."* (*Jour. 1874, 983.*)

OFFICIAL ORGANS.

[See Pythian Journals.]

OFFICIAL RECEIPT.

1. Legislation creating it.

2. Form of.

3. Legal effect of.

(1) Legislation creating it.

235. Much trouble and difficulty having from time to time occurred from the want of an authoritative receipt, which shall, upon its face, not only show the payment of all claims of the Lodge against a brother, but also be authoritative evidence to the Order throughout the World, not only of membership, but good standing in the Order, it was, in 1875, enacted by the Supreme Lodge that the Supreme Chancellor and the Supreme Keeper of Records and Seal issue receipts, which shall be furnished to all Grand and Subordinate Lodges at $2 per 100; and that no receipt shall be authoritative or evidence of payment of dues, assessments or other claims of the Lodge against a member of a Subordinate Lodge, unless written upon such receipt, and bearing the seal of the Supreme Lodge; and that such receipt go into effect on and after July 1, 1875. (*Jour. 1875, 1165.*)

(2) Form of.
(face.)

Official Receipt for Dues	Not genuine unless bearing on its back the seal of the Supreme Lodge and signature of the Supreme Keeper of Records and Seal.

No........ .... LODGE, NO. .... K. OF P.

.... *187..*

Received of Brother ....

Dues from ....*187..to*....................*187..* $........

Assessments ....

Widows and Orphans' Fund............................... ....

Other Claims ....

$........

Impress Lodge Seal on this Receipt.   *Master of Finance.*

(*By-Laws S. L., Const. S. L. 1876, 26.*)

(BACK.)

Office of the Supreme Keeper of Records and Seal,

Columbus, Ohio, June 24, 1875, Pythian Period XII.

At the Seventh Annual Session of the Supreme Lodge Knights of Pythias of the World, held in the city of Washington, Grand Jurisdiction of the District of Columbia, May 18, 19, 20, 21 and 22, 1875, the following was adopted:

"WHEREAS, Much trouble and difficulty has from time to time occurred from the want of an authoritative receipt, which shall, upon its face, not only show the payment of all claims of the Lodge against a brother, but also be authoritative evidence to the Order throughout the world, not only of membership, but good standing in the Order; therefore be it

"*Resolved*, That the Supreme Chancellor and Supreme Keeper of Records and Seal be and hereby are authorized to issue receipts, which shall be furnished to all Grand and Subordinate Lodges at $2 per 100; and that no receipt shall be authoritative or evidence of payment of dues, assessments or other claims of the Lodge against a member of a Subordinate Lodge, unless written upon such receipt, and bearing the seal of the Supreme Lodge.

"*Resolved*, That the receipt above mentioned go into effect on and after July 1, 1875."

　　　　　　　　　　　JOSEPH DOWDALL,
　　　　　　　　Supreme Keeper of Records and Seal.

SEAL SUPREME LODGE KNIGHTS OF PYTHIAS

(*Id. 27.*)

(3) LEGAL EFFECT OF.

236. The official receipt is not only the "usual evidence of good standing," but conclusive evidence thereof. (*Jour. 1876, 1227, 1296.*)

237. Only the official receipt can be recognized as legal. (*Jour. 1876, 1227, 1296.*)

PAGE.

[See Rank; Dues; also clause 7 under Withdrawal Cards.]

PARADES.

[See Funerals; Uniform. Regalia. etc.; Miscellaneous Decisions, under Uniform.]

238. The Supreme Chancellor has no power to order a grand demonstration or parade of the Order in the city of Philadelphia in 1876, nor is it a matter upon which the Supreme Lodge should legislate. Any Subordinate Lodge desiring to appear at such a time should obtain a dispensation from the Grand Chancellor of its jurisdiction. (*Jour. 1874, 933.*)

"PASS" AND "RAISE."
[See " Prove " and " Charge."]

PASSWORDS.
[See Dues ; Supreme Lodge ; Shield.]

239. The Supreme Chancellor shall have exclusive right of creation and promulgation of all passwords proper and fitting for the case involved; to rescind, call in and change the same, if circumstances require or the exigencies of the case warrant; prescribe their application and use. (*Const., Art. xvi.*)

240. The Supreme Chancellor can rescind the S. A. P. W. of a Grand Jurisdiction if the exigencies of the case demand it. (*Jour. 1875, 1115, 1116.*)

241. A Chancellor Commander can communicate the S. A. P. W. only to members of his own Lodge, except on an order from the Chancellor Commander of some Lodge in the same jurisdiction, under seal of his Lodge and attested by the K. of R. and S. (*Jour. 1875, 1042, 1114.*)

242. This decision was in 1876 explained and modified by the Supreme Chancellor, who stated that it was intended that a Chancellor Commander should be empowered to instruct the members of his Lodge in the S. A. P. W.; also, all members in or out of his jurisdiction presenting an order for it, under seal of his Lodge, signed by the Chancellor Commander and attested by the K. of R. and S., and presenting the usual evidence of his good standing. (*Jour. 1876, 1228.*)

243. A Chancellor Commander may require a visiting member presenting an order for the S. A. P. W. to show a receipt for dues before instructing him in the word. A receipt should always accompany an order for the S. A. P.W. Only the official receipt can be recognized as legal. (*Jour. 1876, 1227, 1296.*)

244. But a visiting member who is in possession of the S. A. P. W. cannot be required before entering a Lodge to produce a receipt for dues, and be examined in the secret work. (*Jour. 1876, 1227, 1296.*)

245. The Lodge, or its officers, has the right, and it is their duty, to refuse admission to any one unless in posses- sion of the S. A. P. W., as also the ante-rooms must be cleared of all who are without it, be they members or can- didates, so that the Outer Steward has complete control of who enters, unless otherwise ordered by the Worthy Chan- cellor. (*Jour. 1873, App. 38.*)

246. The term P. W. is to be communicated to Knights only. (*Jour. 1870, 229.*)

247. The S. A. P. W. cannot be used, given or taken in any degree but that of Knight, except it be in opening at the outer door, or in examining the Lodge preparatory to passing from the Page or Esquire degree to that of Knight; yet the Lodge has — or its official head the Worthy Chan- cellor — the right to exact the S. A. P. W. whenever and wherever it deems the safety of the work requires, or any doubt exists as to propriety of proceeding without it, as an evidence in good standing in the Order and privilege of attending, etc.; but it cannot exact from the Page or Esquire that which they are not in possession of, they not having been invested with it. (*Jour. 1873, App. 38.*)

248. It is competent for the C. C. to instruct the M. at A. to receive the P. W. in the ante-room after each of the visiting Knights have worked their way through the outer door; and a Lodge, as a body, can thus be admitted to the Castle Hall of a Lodge in session without the P. W. being given by each individual member at the inner door. (*Jour. 1874, 913, 935.*)

249. A brother having a withdrawal card is entitled to the P. W. current at the time of withdrawal, and should he fail to attach himself to a Lodge during the continuance of that word, he is not entitled to receive a subsequent P. W. until he has joined a Lodge. (*Jour. 1871, 327; 1872, 467; 1875, 1160.*)

250. The A. S. W. is the only universal P.W. which can be communicated to those holding an unexpired traveling shield, excepting always the proper Grand and Subordinate Lodge officers; the S. A. P. W. must be local in its use; a different one for each Grand Jurisdiction and territory where no Grand Lodge existed; and dues to be paid for the full time covered by the A. S. Ws. required by the time specified in the shield. (*Jour. 1875, 1017.*) For the old legislation on the subject, see *Jour. 1868, 18; 1869, 67, 101.*)

The rule stated in this section (250) was changed in 1875, and the S. A. P. W. is now universal, and, in connection with the usual evidence of good standing, is sufficient to admit any brother into any Lodge of the Order. (*See post, Sec. 305.*)

251. **Art. XI** of the [old] Supreme Lodge Constitution, providing that "any Grand Lodge neglecting to forward its returns, together with the representative tax due previous to the annual session of the Supreme Lodge, shall disqualify its members from voting in the Supreme Lodge, and shall not be entitled to receive the P. W. until said returns and payments are made," refers to the current P. Ws., and not the Supreme Lodge P. W.   (*Jour. 1874, 859.*)

PAST CHANCELLORS.
[See Subordinate Lodges.]

PAST GRAND CHANCELLOR.
[See Grand Lodge.]

"PROVE" AND "CHARGE."

252. **The use** of the words "passed" and "raised" being inapplicable to this Order, was in 1871 abjured by the Supreme Lodge, and all Grand and Subordinate Lodges of the Order were recommended to abjure and drop the use of said words, and substitute therefor the words "prove" and "charge" in all official documents, dispensations or charters thereafter issued, as also recommend said rectification to those already issued, wherever possible or practicable so to do.   (*Jour. 1871, 365, 385.*)

PYTHIAN JOURNALS.

253. **The Supreme Lodge** recognizes the powerful aid of the press of our land in building up and maintaining our beloved Order, and recommends and enjoins on our membership the propriety of encouraging our Pythian journals in every legitimate manner. (*Jour. 1876, 1311.*)

254. While the Supreme Lodge is pleased to encourage all reputable publications in the interest of the Order, it does not recognize any publication, of whatever name, as its official organ. (*Jour. 1873, 721; 1870, 221.*)

See certain journals recognized as "organs of the Order" in Jour. 1868, 59; 1870, 221.

PYTHIAN PERIOD.
[See Anniversary.]

255. The Order having been inaugurated and established in the year A.D. 1864, it was enacted at the session of 1871 that thereafter the term "Pythian Period" should be used immediately after any date given of day, year or month of the vulgar era, as follows: "This the —— day of ——, A.D. 18—, and of Pythian Period the ——," in all official documents, dispensations or charters emanating from or issued by the Supreme Lodge or Grand Lodges under its jurisdiction; and that the date of the Pythian Period should date back and commence on the 19th February, 1864, and that each and every year thereafter and to come should succeed in regular numerical order, commencing on the 19th day of February of each year. (*Jour. 1871, 364, 385.*)

RAFFLE.
[See Lotteries.]

RANK CREDENTIALS.
[See Withdrawal Cards.]

RANKS AND TITLES.
1. Terms "degree" etc.
2. Interval between conferring.
3. Pages and Esquires.
[See Membership; Honors; Withdrawal Cards.]

(1) TERMS "DEGREE" ETC.

256. At the session of the Supreme Lodge in 1872 the word "degree" and "degrees" was ordered to be struck out wherever appearing in the Ritual, Laws, Installations or Odes, or when used in connection with the Order of Knights of Pythias, or its legislation and workings, and the word "rank" inserted in its or their place. (*Jour. 1872, 561, 598.*)

257. The title "Sir Knight" should not be used in designating members of the Order of Knights of Pythias. (*Jour. 1872, 564, 598.*)

(2) Interval between Conferring.

258. One week must elapse between the conferring of the ranks in all cases, except the first four meetings of a new Lodge; but in every instance one week must elapse between the application and the conferring of the initiatory rank of Page.

The above paragraph shall not apply to cases where dispensations are granted by a proper Grand Officer, or through his deputy. [Obligatory.] (*Const., Art. viii, Sec. 2.*)

(3) Pages and Esquires.
[See Withdrawal Cards.]

259. Pages and Esquires are entitled to and can be admitted in a Lodge when opened and working in that rank. (*Jour. 1873, App. 38.*)

They can pass the outer door, if having to do so by the order of the Chancellor Commander. (*Jour. 1873, App. 38.*)

260. The law makes Pages members of the Order; but their rights as to full membership for all purposes vary in different jurisdictions, and it is inadvisable to have withdrawal cards for any members but Knights. (*Jour. 1874, 933. See, also, Withdrawal Cards.*)

261. Charges cannot be preferred against a member who, having received the ranks of Page and Esquire, proceeds through a portion of the Knight's rank, and refuses to proceed any farther with that rank. The Esquire is, however, not entitled to any benefits, privileges or honors of the Knight's rank. (*Jour. 1875, 1133, 1140.*)

262. A Subordinate Lodge may confer the ranks of Esquire and Knight on a Page who has received that rank in another Lodge, in the same or another jurisdiction, by a written official request of his Lodge, certifying that he has received the rank of Page, and has paid for the other ranks, and been elected thereto. The Lodge conferring those ranks should, when the rank or ranks are conferred, send to the Lodge making the request an official notice of the ranks having been conferred, with date, and he should be entered on their books holding rank accordingly. (*Jour. 1875, 1043, 1114.*)

RECEIPTS.
[See Official Receipts.]

REGALIA.
[See Uniform.]

- RELIEF FUNDS.
[See Benefits, etc.; Insurance ; Committees.]

REPORTS.
[See Supreme Lodge and its Officers, under the heads Supreme Chancellor, Supreme Master of Exchequer, Supreme Keeper of Records and Seal.]

263. Supreme Representatives' written reports to their Grand Lodges or Grand Officers are official in so far as rendering a Supreme law operative in its effect prior to the issuance of the Journal of Proceedings or a General Order, and may be recognized until said Journal of Proceedings or General Orders are issued, when said general promulgation and issuance of the Journal or Orders, if differing in their reports in letter, spirit or construction, it (Journal or Orders) must be immediately conformed to in every respect. (*Const., Art. xv.*)

264. The Reports of the Supreme Chancellor and Supreme Keeper of Records and Seal are to be printed previous to the annual sessions. (*Jour. 1870, 219.*)

265. For a Grand Lodge to mutilate the report of its Grand Chancellor when it contains no objectionable language, nor any matter connected with the private work of the Order, is a wrong and injustice. (*Jour. 1870, 199.*)

6

RESIDENCE.
[See Membership.]

RESIGNATIONS.
[See Vacancies.]

266. The Installation Ceremonies requiring a Grand Chancellor, and that officer only to obligate himself to perform the duties of his office for the present term, he can resign at will during the term. (*Jour. 1872, 564, 585.*)

267. The First Ven. Patriarch can resign. (*Jour. 1872, 620, 630.*)

This would read Past Chancellor under the new titles.

RETURNS.
[See, also, Supreme Lodge ; Delinquent or Defunct Lodges ; Passwords ; Reports.]

268. Each Grand Lodge under the control of the Supreme Lodge, as also all Subordinate Lodges in any State, Country, Island or Territory where there is no Grand Lodge legally at work or properly instituted, shall make out annual returns of its work and business in accordance with the form sent or delivered to them by the Supreme Keeper of Records and Seal, or other proper officer, and forward the same, with the legal dues or tax from that body to the Supreme Lodge, to said Supreme Keeper of Records and Seal, on or before the first day of May of each year, or, in default thereof, such Grand Lodge shall forfeit its right to representation at the next session of the Supreme Lodge. (*Const., Art. xviii.*)

[See Jour. 1868, 18.]

269. At the session of 1873 the Supreme Lodge adopted the following resolution, which, with the proper changes as to the names of officers, seems still to be applicable:

"*Resolved*, That the Supreme Lodge furnish the Grand Recording and Corresponding Scribe of each Grand Jurisdiction, and Deputy Grand Chancellor where no Grand Lodge exists, printed blanks to report to the Supreme Chancellor, Supreme Recording and Corresponding Scribe

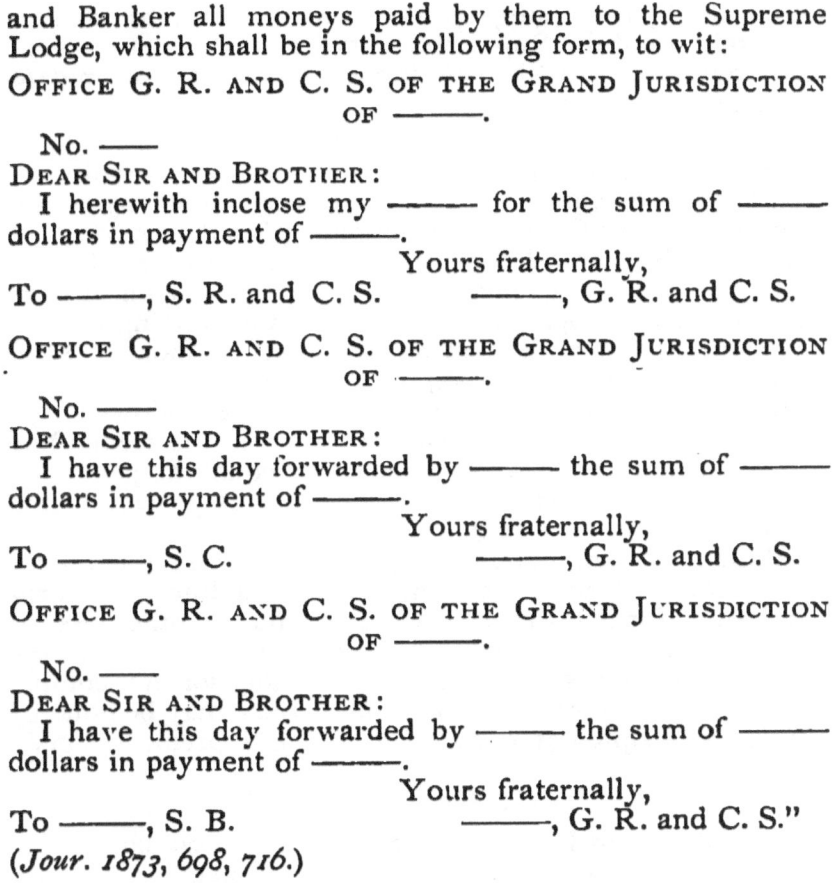

and Banker all moneys paid by them to the Supreme Lodge, which shall be in the following form, to wit:

OFFICE G. R. AND C. S. OF THE GRAND JURISDICTION
OF ———.

No. ——
DEAR SIR AND BROTHER:
I herewith inclose my ——— for the sum of ———
dollars in payment of ———.

Yours fraternally,

To ———, S. R. and C. S.   ———, G. R. and C. S.

OFFICE G. R. AND C. S. OF THE GRAND JURISDICTION
OF ———.

No. ——
DEAR SIR AND BROTHER:
I have this day forwarded by ——— the sum of ———
dollars in payment of ———.

Yours fraternally,

To ———, S. C.   ———, G. R. and C. S.

OFFICE G. R. AND C. S. OF THE GRAND JURISDICTION
OF ———.

No. ——
DEAR SIR AND BROTHER:
I have this day forwarded by ——— the sum of ———
dollars in payment of ———.

Yours fraternally,

To ———, S. B.   ———, G. R. and C. S."

(*Jour. 1873, 698, 716.*)

REVENUE.

1. Of Supreme Lodge.
2. Of Grand Lodges.
3. Of Subordinate Lodges.

[See, also, Supreme Lodge ; Supreme Master of Exchequer and Supreme Keeper of Records and Seal, in Supreme Lodge ; Committee ; Subordinate Lodges.]

(1) OF SUPREME LODGE.

270. Each Grand Lodge shall pay to the Supreme Lodge the sum of $75 annually for each representative to which they are entitled, and each Grand and Subordinate

Lodge shall pay for supplies such sums as may be fixed in the By-Laws of the Supreme Lodge; and all work or supplies so ordered must be paid for when ordering, or on date of delivery. (*Const., Art. x.*)

[See Supplies.]

271. **It is doubtful** whether revenue can lawfully be raised for the Supreme Lodge by assessment upon the members of each Grand Jurisdiction. (*Jour. 1874, 979.*)

And the Supreme Lodge, by its refusal to adopt the following amendments, offered in 1875 and acted upon in 1876, showed their disapproval of any legislation looking toward its maintenance by a system of direct taxation. (*Jour. 1875, 1167; 1876, 1324, 1329.*)

"Amend paragraph 6 of Sec. 1 of Art. I, as follows:

"Add, after the words 'furnished by it,' in the second line of the paragraph, the words 'and by an equal tax per capita upon the whole membership, when the exigencies of the Supreme Lodge require it.'

"Amend by adding, in paragraph 6, Sec. 1, Art. I, after the words 'Grand Lodge,' in the second line, the words 'and such further direct tax per capita, or otherwise, as may at any time be deemed necessary, and provide the mode of collecting the same, and penalty for non-compliance or non-payment of the same, which may be done by resolution adopted at any session of the Supreme Lodge.'"

(2) OF GRAND LODGES.

272. A Grand Lodge may require a Subordinate Lodge to pay a per capita tax on suspended members. (*Jour. 1870, 180, 206.*)

It was decided at the same session that a brother suspended for non-payment of dues ceases to be a member of the Order till reinstated. (*Jour. 1870, 225.*)

273. No Grand Lodge has power to levy assessments on Past Chancellors and refuse to admit such as refuse to pay the same. (*Jour. 1870, 203.*)

274. On appeal against the action of the Grand Lodge of Maryland, in passing the following resolution — "That the levy of per capita tax for the year 1875 shall be at the rate of 25 cents per member, semi-annually; one-fifth of the amount to be made a sinking fund to aid in the purpose of building a Pythian Castle, and in the event of the building not being commenced in five years, the amount paid in by each Lodge, and the interest which has accrued thereon, shall be returned to it,"—which resolution was objected to on the ground of the proviso that one-fifth of the amount be retained for the purpose of building a Hall for the Order: *Held*, that the resolution was in accordance with the Constitution of the Grand Lodge of Maryland, and the appeal was dismissed. (*Jour. 1875, 1148.*)

275. Money paid by a Lodge to a Deputy Grand Chancellor duly authorized to receive the same, cannot be again required of the Lodge. (*Jour. 1868, 46, 47.*)

(3) OF SUBORDINATE LODGES.
[See Dues.]

276. A Subordinate Lodge can levy a tax on its members to meet the necessary expenses of the Lodge if approved by the Grand Lodge, that being a matter belonging to local legislation. (*Jour. 1872, 625.*)

RITUAL.

1. Amplified Ritual.
2. Exchange of imperfect Rituals.
3. Translations of.
4. Where to be kept.
5. Memorizing Ritual.
6. Copying prohibited.
7. Acroatic Agenda.
8. Preamble to revised Ritual.

[See Supreme Lodge.]

(1) AMPLIFIED RITUAL.

277. At the session of 1872 an amplified Third Degree was adopted, and the Supreme Scribe instructed to have the Rituals bound both with and without the Amplified Degree, and Grand and Subordinate Lodges were authorized to order whichever they desired, and that a difference be made in the price proportionate to the cost of printing. (*Jour. 1872, 609.*)

278. A Subordinate Lodge has an unqualified right to

determine for itself, and to demand the Amplified Ritual. (*Jour. 1873, 718.*)

(2) EXCHANGE OF IMPERFECT RITUALS.

279. In 1874 it was *Resolved,* "That the Supreme Recording and Corresponding Scribe be directed to exchange all copies of imperfect Rituals, which may have been issued *to* and *are now* in the hands of Subordinate or Grand Lodges, for copies in proper condition, without extra charge." (*Jour. 1874, 902, 936.*)

(3) TRANSLATIONS OF.

280. Various provisions have from time to time been made for the production of Rituals in foreign languages for the use of the Order. (*Jour. 1871, 261, 379, 382, 386; 1872, 620; 1874, 853, 936.*)

(4) WHERE TO BE KEPT.

281. The proper place for the keeping of the Rituals and other private work is in the Castle Halls of the Order; and it is the duty of the Lodge to provide a suitable box or other receptacle, with a sufficient lock, the key of which shall be in the charge and keeping of the Chancellor Commander; and it is his duty to prevent their removal from the Castle Hall. (*Jour. 1875, 1152.*)

(5) MEMORIZING RITUAL.

282. The Third or Knight's degree shall in no instance be conferred according to the Second or Amplified Ritual of said degree as adopted, unless the various parts have been memorized by all the persons officiating therein, so that the same can be conferred without the use of the book. (*Jour. 1872, 637.*)

283. While it is essential to the welfare and influence of the Order that all of the lectures and charges should, where the same is practicable, be memorized, yet there are times and seasons when the same (if made imperative) would hinder and delay the business of Subordinate Lodges; and it is recommended that the several Grand Jurisdictions be requested to use their best efforts to procure the memorizing of all lectures and charges upon the part of officers of Subordinate Lodges. (*Jour. 1875, 1153.*)

284. **There** being no general law bearing upon the memorizing of the ritualistic charges, it rests clearly in the province of the Subordinate Lodge to declare in what space of time the officer *shall*, by memorizing, be able to deliver the same "orally." (*Jour. 1873, App. 37.*)

285. **Under** the decision of the Supreme Chancellor, on page 37 of his report, Jour. 1873 (*supra*), regarding the memorizing of charges by officers, it will not be competent for a Grand Chancellor to require that the officers of Lodges in his jurisdiction shall memorize the ritualistic charges of their office within a specified time after their installation, and that at the expiration of that time the Rituals shall be delivered by the Lodges to their District Deputy Grand Chancellors, to be retained by them until the next installation of officers. (*Jour. 1873, 756.*) .

(6) COPYING PROHIBITED.

286. **All officers** and members of Subordinate Lodges are prohibited from copying, in any manner, any part or parts of their several charges, or other ritualistic ceremonies. (*Jour. 1875, 1134.*)

(7) ACROATIC AGENDA.

287. **The "Acroatic Agendas"** are *not* Lodge property. They are only issued by the Supreme Lodge to proper officers to harmonize the *whole* work of the Order, and subject to recall at any time that it may order. (*Jour. 1873, App. 37.*)

(8) THE PREAMBLE TO THE REVISED RITUAL AS ADOPTED AT THE SESSION OF 1872.

[Jour. 1872, 601, 656.]

288. WHEREAS, The Order of Knights of Pythias, now numbering nearly one thousand Subordinate, twenty-eight Grand and one Supreme Lodge, with a membership of nearly or quite one hundred thousand, have, in their Ritualistic Ceremonials as now practiced, many contradictions and anachronisms of a nature calculated to mar and destroy the beautiful and valuable teachings sought to be inculcated thereby; and

WHEREAS, By its name as an Order we are led to suppose that it was founded upon the tradition of, and what tran-

spired during, the life of and between those two great historic
characters, "Damon and Pythias;" and

WHEREAS, The *prefix* "Knight" establishes the supposi-
tious belief and implied understanding that it was intended
to be and *is* an Order of *a semi*-military and chivalric character; and

WHEREAS, All pertaining to such an Order should, both
in its Titles, Name, Usages and Ritualistic Ceremonials,
carry out and conform thereto, as also blend in the Names,
Principles and Lessons as conceived from the great life
drama that as an Order it is intended to perpetuate; therefore be it

Resolved, Ordained and Ordered, By this Supreme Legislative and Executive Head of the Order of K. of P., in
solemn convention assembled, that the hereinafter revised,
corrected, altered, amplified and amended Ritual of Ceremonies, for the use of *all* Subordinate Lodges K. of P. now
in existence, or hereafter established of the Order of K. of
P., under the jurisdiction of the various Grand Lodges com-
prising or under the special jurisdiction of this Supreme
Lodge K. of P. of the World, be and the same is hereby
adopted. And be it further

Resolved, That the Supreme Chancellor and Supreme R.
and C. S. be and they are hereby authorized and ordered to
have a sufficient quantity of this revised, corrected, altered,
amplified and amended Ritual, with its accompanying diagrams, plates, notes, references, change in and increase of
work, and auxiliary lectures, printed, to supply the place of
the form of Ritual now in use by all of said Subordinate
Lodges K. of P., as hereinfore mentioned and set forth,
as also sufficient for any increase of Lodges that may occur
prior to the next session of this Supreme Body; and be it
further

Resolved, That the Supreme Chancellor and Supreme R.
and C. S. of this Supreme Lodge of the World shall furnish said revised, corrected, altered, amplified and amended
Rituals through the different Grand Lodges and their
proper officers to said Subordinate Lodges in whose Grand
Jurisdiction they may be situate, and to all Subordinate
Lodges now held under the special jurisdiction of this Supreme Lodge at minimum rate of $1 per copy, or $5 per
set, and in exchange for those of the form now in use, when

this present form as now adopted are issued and officially promulgated; and be it further

Resolved, That on and after the 1st day of July, A.D. 1872, and of P. P. the 9th, or so soon thereafter as is possible, that all of the present form of Ritual of Ceremonial now in use shall be called in by the Supreme R. and C. S. through the proper Grand Officers of the various Grand Jurisdictions, and be replaced in the same sources by the form now adopted; and which called in Rituals, or those of that form that may be on hand, shall be destroyed by the Supreme Chancellor and Supreme R. and C. S., or other properly delegated authority by them; and be it further

Resolved, That after thirty days from the hereinafter date of official issuance and promulgation, the use of the said herein adopted, revised, corrected, altered, amplified and amended Ritual, and appended Work and Lectures, *shall* be obligatory, and the use of the present form become illegal in its use, under the pains and penalties of the law as made and provided by the Grand Lodges in whose various jurisdictions Lodges may be situate, or of this Supreme Lodge of K. of P. of the World; and be it further

Resolved, That otherwise than as herein expressed the legislation of this Supreme Lodge, whether constitutional or otherwise, be and the same is hereby continued in force, but all other matters pertaining to or in conflict herewith be and the same is hereby repealed; and be it finally

Resolved, That from and after the adoption of this hereinafter revised, corrected, altered, amplified and amended Ritual of Ceremonials and appendant Work for the use of Subordinate Lodges of the Order of K. of P., no alteration, amendment or other change shall be made in the same for the space of ——— years, or until the regular session of A.D. 18—, and of P. P. the ———.

From the Journal it appears that the Supreme Lodge decided to have all old Rituals recalled and returned to the different Grand R. and C. Ss., to be then forwarded by them to the Supreme R. and C. S. *prior* to the 1st of July, 1872, the new Ritual, with the key, being furnished all Lodges to replace those now in use; and that thereafter the price or prices remain as fixed by the Supreme Lodge. (*Jour. 1872, 560, 602.*)

289. **The names and titles** of the officers of a Subordinate Lodge of Knights of Pythias shall be as follows:

1. *Past Chancellor.*—Acquired by service and after having passed through the executive office and chair of the Lodge, and which title and rank shall be held thereafter.

2. *Chancellor Commander*, which latter title of *Commander* shall only be held and worn while the principal and executive officer of the Lodge, and *no longer*.

3. *Vice Chancellor.*
4. *Prelate.*
5. *Master of Exchequer.*
6. *Master of Finance.*
7. *Keeper of Records & Seal.*
8. *Master-at-Arms.*
9. *Inner Guard.*
10. *Outer Guard.*

OFFICERS AND THEIR DUTIES.

Past Chancellor, who is the retiring Chancellor Commander, to have charge of, and be held responsible for, *all* preparations of and for floor work, or Ceremonials in conferring the degrees, or any other duties detailed for him to do by the Chancellor Commander when the Lodge is working.

Chancellor Commander, who is the *chief* executive officer of the Lodge, whose duties are those as now prescribed for the Worthy Chancellors of Lodges.

Vice Chancellor, who is the *second* executive officer of the Lodge, whose duties are those as now prescribed for that office.

Prelate, who is the *third* executive officer of the Lodge, whose duties shall be those as formerly prescribed for and pertaining to the office of and known as Ven. Patriarch.

Master of Exchequer.— Same as formerly prescribed for the B.

Master of Finance.— Same as formerly prescribed for the F. S.

Keeper of Records and Seal.— Same as formerly prescribed for the R. and C. S.

Master-at-Arms.— Same as formerly prescribed for the G.

Inner Guard.— Same as formerly prescribed for the I. S.

Outer Guard.— Same as formerly prescribed for the O. S.

OFFICES, HOW ATTAINED.

Past Chancellor.— By service in the chairs.
Chancellor Commander.— By election.
Vice Chancellor.— By election.
Prelate.— By election.
Master of Exchequer.— By election.
Master of Finance.— By election.
Keeper of Records and Seal.— By election.

Master-at-Arms.— By election or appointment.

Inner Guard.— By appointment.

Outer Guard.— By appointment.

OFFICERS AND THEIR POSITIONS.

Past Chancellor.— On the *right* hand side of Lodge, midway or center of room, looking from the Chancellor Commander's station to the Vice Chancellor at the opposite end.

Chancellor Commander.—At *head* or end of room.

Vice Chancellor.—At the *opposite* or lower end of room.

Prelate.— On *left* hand side of the Chancellor Commander, at center of Lodge and in a direct line as drawn from the Past Chancellor over or through the Altar opposite the position of the Past Chancellor.

Master of Exchequer and *Master of Finance.*—At head of Lodge room and on the *left* of the Chancellor Commander.

Keeper of Records and Seals and *Master at Arms.*—At head of the Lodge room and on the *right* of the Chancellor Commander.

Inner Guard.—At inner door and near the Vice Chancellor.

Outer Guard.—At outer door.

DIAGRAM SHOWING THE POSITION OF THE OFFICERS AND THE SHAPE OF THEIR STATIONS AND THEIR COLORS:

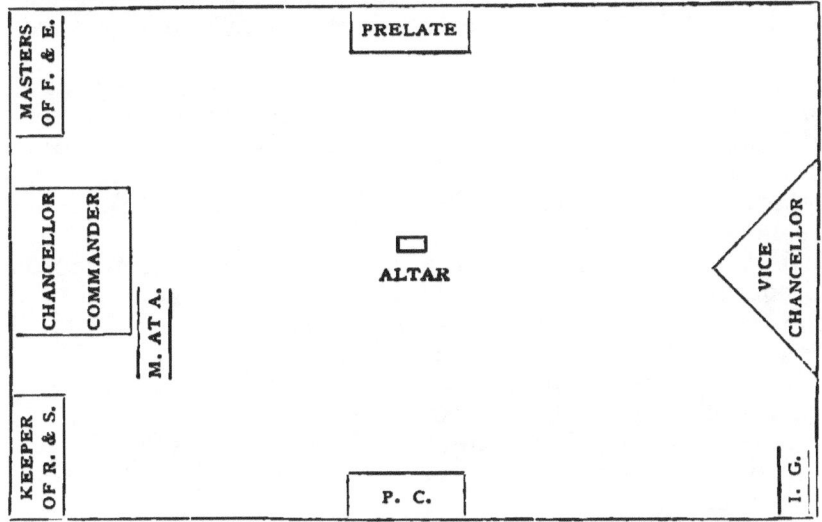

V. C., blue.   P., black.   C. C., red.   P. C., yellow.

RULES OF ORDER OF SUPREME LODGE.

290. 1. The presiding officer having taken the chair, the officers and members shall take their respective seats, and at the sound of the gavel there shall be a general silence.

2. At the appointed hour the Supreme Chancellor shall organize the meeting by directing the Supreme Keeper of Records and Seal to call the names of the officers of this Supreme Lodge. After which he shall make report of the number of Grand Lodges from which Representatives are present; when, if a quorum be present, the Supreme Chancellor shall call on the Supreme Prelate to address the Supreme Ruler of the Universe in prayer. The Supreme Vice Chancellor and the Supreme Master at Arms shall then examine the Representatives present, and report to the Supreme Chancellor, and, if correct, the Supreme Chancellor shall direct the members to clothe themselves with their regalia and take their seats, after which the Supreme Vice Chancellor, at the request of the Supreme Chancellor, shall proclaim the Lodge duly opened.

3. The business shall be taken up in the following order: The Supreme Lodge shall be opened in due form.

4. The Supreme Keeper of Records and Seal will report on the certificates of Representatives, which shall be referred to the proper committee.

5. The Supreme Chancellor shall appoint a Committee on Credentials and Returns, and a Committee on Allotment of Seats — each committee to consist of five members. Both of said committees shall report without delay, and said reports shall be acted upon and disposed of before any other business is transacted.

6. On the adoption of the report of the Committee on Credentials and Returns, recommending the admission of the Past Grand Chancellors and representatives, they shall be admitted in form.

7. The minutes of the last annual and intervening meetings shall be read and passed upon.

8. The report of the Supreme Chancellor, as to his acts and doings during the recess of the Supreme Lodge, shall be presented.

9. The annual reports of the Supreme Keeper of Records

and Seal, and Supreme Master of Exchequer, shall be presented.

10. The Supreme Chancellor shall then appoint the following committees, each to consist of five members, viz.:

Committee on Law and Supervision.
Committee on Finance.
Committee on Appeals and Grievances.
Committee on Mileage.
Committee on State of the Order.
Committee on Written Work.
Committee on Unwritten Work.
Committee on Printing.
Committee on Dispensations and Charters.

11. The Jurisdictions shall be called in their order of seniority, when any legitimate business may be presented.

12. Petitions shall be presented, read and referred.

13. Reports of Standing Committees to be called by the Supreme Chancellor in the order of their appointment.

14. Reports of Special Committees.

15. Miscellaneous Business.

16. The above order of business may be transposed or dispensed with, at the discretion of the Supreme Lodge. When the business of the session is concluded, the Supreme Prelate shall offer a prayer, and the Supreme Vice Chancellor shall proclaim the Supreme Lodge duly closed.

17. Voting for officers shall be by ballot. All other voting shall be *viva voce*, or by yeas and nays, as the Supreme Lodge may determine.

18. On the call of two jurisdictions, the yeas and nays shall be taken on any question, and when taken shall be entered on the Journal.

19. No motion shall be subject to debate until it has been seconded and stated by the Chair. It shall be reduced to writing at the request of any member.

20. When a question is before the Supreme Lodge, no motion shall be received, unless it be to adjourn, the previous question, to lie on the table, to refer, to postpone indefinitely, to postpone to a certain time, to recommit, or to amend; and the motions just enumerated shall take precedence in the order of enumeration. The first three shall be decided without debate.

21. When a subject has been indefinitely postponed, it

cannot again, during the same session, be taken up and considered; nor can a subject which the Supreme Lodge has refused to reconsider, be taken up at that session.

22. On a call of Representatives of three Grand Jurisdictions, a majority of the Supreme Lodge may demand that the previous question shall be put, which shall always be in this form: "*Shall the main question be now put?*" and, until it is decided, no further debate shall take place, and the vote shall be taken, first, on any amendments that may be pending, and next on the final question.

23. When the reading of any paper or other matter is called for, and the same is objected to by any member, it shall be determined by vote of the Supreme Lodge without debate.

24. Before putting a question, the presiding officer shall ask, "*Is the Supreme Lodge ready for the question?*" If no member rise to speak, and a majority of the Supreme Lodge are ready for the question, he shall rise and put it. While the presiding officer is putting a question, or addressing the Supreme Lodge, none shall walk out of or across the room, nor entertain private discourse; and after he shall have risen to put it, no member shall speak upon it.

25. The presiding officer, or any other member doubting the decision of a question, may call for a division of the Supreme Lodge, but a division cannot be called for after the Chair has announced the result of a vote.

26. No member shall be permitted to speak or vote unless clothed in regalia according to his rank and station, and occupying his seat at the place designated for him.

27. During the progress of a ballot for an officer no motion can be entertained, or debate or explanation permitted.

28. Every officer and member shall be designated by his proper title or office according in the Order.

29. Every member, when he speaks or offers a motion, shall rise and respectfully address and be recognized by the presiding officer; and while speaking he shall confine himself to the question in debate, avoiding all personalities and indecorous language, as well as all reflections upon the Supreme Lodge or any of its members.

30. Should two or more members rise to speak at the same time, the Chair shall decide which is entitled to the floor; and no member shall interrupt or disturb another

while speaking, unless to call him to order for words spoken.

31. If a member, while speaking, shall be called to order, he shall, at the request of the Chair, take his seat until the question of order is determined, when he may proceed again.

32. The decisions of the Chair on points of order may be appealed from by any member, which point of order shall be reduced to writing; and in such cases the question shall be, "*Shall the decision of the Chair stand as the judgment of the Supreme Lodge?*"

33. No member shall speak more than once on the same question until all the members wishing to speak have had an opportunity to do so; and no one shall speak more than ten minutes on any question, unless by permission of the Supreme Lodge.

34. When a petition, memorial or communication is presented, a brief statement of its contents shall be made by the introducer or the Chair; and, after it has been read, a brief notice of its purport shall be entered upon the Journal.

35. When a blank is to be filled, the question shall be taken first upon the highest sum or number, and the longest or latest time proposed.

36. Any member may call for the division of a question, when the sense will admit.

37. After any question, except one of indefinite postponement, or one which the Supreme Lodge has refused to reconsider, has been decided, any two members who voted in the majority, may, at the same or next session, move for a reconsideration thereof; but no discussion of the main question shall be allowed until reconsidered.

38. No matter shall be considered at any morning session of the Supreme Lodge until all the committees shall have had an opportunity of presenting reports.

39. A committee appointed at one session to perform a duty are bound to report, although some of the members of the committee have ceased to be members of this body.

40. Any member has a right to protest, and to have an epitome of his protest spread upon the Journal, if in respectful language.

41. Every member is bound to vote, serve on committees, and accept nominations, unless excused by vote.

42. No member shall be allowed to cast his vote after a ballot has been announced.

43. No more than two amendments to a proposition shall be entertained at the same time; that is, an amendment and an amendment to an amendment, and the question shall be first taken on the latter.

44. Any proposition offered for reference to any standing or special committee of this body, which shall require an entry in full upon the Journal, shall be submitted in duplicate, either in print or in manuscript; and, if in writing, they shall be on paper not less in size than half a page of foolscap. All resolutions and legislative measures belonging to or within the purview of any standing or special committee of this body, shall be referred in the regular order to said committees, before reported on and submitted by them for action thereon, by the Supreme Lodge.

45. The Supreme Chancellor shall appoint a Standing Committee on Rules, to whom shall be referred all amendments thereto, and all questions of order not otherwise disposed of.

46. The election of officers shall take place on such day of the session as the Supreme Lodge may determine.

47. The installation of officers shall be after the business of the session, at which the election takes place, has been completed.

48. Cushing's Manual shall be our standard for parliamentary law, in the absence of any rule governing our action.

49. Proposals to add to, amend or alter these rules, shall be submitted in writing and lay over at least one day, when a majority vote shall adopt or reject.
(*Jour. 1875, 1109–1111.*)

SEALS.

1. Of Supreme Lodge.
2. Of Supreme Chancellor.
3. Of Grand and Subordinate Lodges.
[See, also, Supreme K. of R. & S. (in Supreme Lodge); Shields.]

(1) OF SUPREME LODGE.

291. **The seal** is a polygon — five-sided. The five sides represent the five Grand Lodges in existence upon the formation of the Supreme Lodge. On one side, the date of organization of the Supreme Lodge; on the other, the date of the foundation of the Order. Over the shield the word "Friendship," the corner-stone of the Order. On the shield a "flotant," with stars upon it, denoting our ascendancy. The perpendicular lines denote the color "Blue," the dots, "Yellow," the horizontal, "Red," thus showing the colors of the Order. The "*Dirigo*" means "I guide," or "I direct." Around the shield are the initials of the mottoes F., C. and B. (*Jour. 1868, 25, 45, 47.*)

292. The Supreme Lodge seal was copyrighted in 1874 in the name of S. S. Davis, Supreme Chancellor, which action was approved by the Supreme Lodge in 1875. (*Jour. 1871, 382; 1875, 1029, 1134.*)

293. It seems that the use of an imprint seal of the Supreme Lodge is not legal. (*Jour. 1873, App. 13.*)

The recommendation of the Supreme Chancellor on p. 13 of App., in respect to the use of the imprint seal, does not appear to have been acted upon by the Supreme Lodge.

(2) Of Supreme Chancellor.

294. The use, by the Supreme Chancellor, of an individual official seal was in 1873 authorized, though the limits of its use do not seem to have been defined by the Supreme Lodge, though definitely marked out by the Supreme Chancellor in his recommendation. (*See Jour. 1873, 719, 746; App. 14.*)

(3) Of Grand and Subordinate Lodges.

295. All Grand and Subordinate Lodges shall have an appropriate seal bearing proper devices thereon, name, number and location of the Lodge, with the date of its institution thereon, a good copy or impression of which shall be deposited with the Supreme K. of R and S. (*Const., Art. xxvi.*)

296. Each Subordinate Lodge shall have a seal with appropriate devices, which shall be affixed to such cards, as well as to all official documents emanating from the Lodge. [Obligatory.] (*Const., Art. vii, Sec. 2.*)

7

SHIELDS AND ANNUAL SHIELD WORDS.
[See Passwords.]

While the late legislation has practically abolished the shield for the purposes for which it was originally intended, yet the old legislation is here given so that there may be a clear understanding as to its origin and past uses.

297. Traveling shields for the use of brethren can only be used or recognized when procured from the Supreme Lodge, and are of the prescribed and legal form, as adopted, and under its restrictions as made for general or special use, by Grand Lodges, and from them issued to the Subordinate Lodges for issuance to members, *except* it be where no Grand Lodge is in existence, or recognized by this Supreme Lodge, and in such cases from the Deputy Supreme Chancellor in charge of said State or Territory. (*Const., Art. xxix.*)

298. The Supreme Chancellor was instructed by legislation, in 1874, to create *annually* an annual shield *Password*, which said A. S.W. shall accompany said shield when issued to a member, to be used by him for purposes thereon indicated, and none else; and the presentation of " Shield " *without* the " A. S.W.," or " A. S.W." *without* the " Shield," in either case are worthless for the object sought to be attained, but must be presented *together* to be of value, and operative in the sense for and in which presented. (*Jour. 1874, 969.*)

299. The A.S.W. shall be promulgated by the Supreme Chancellor, in the usual course and manner, through the various Grand and Deputy Supreme Chancellors of the different jurisdictions, to the Chancellor Commander of each and every Lodge of the Order, wherever existing, and in turn said Chancellor Commander shall invest the *actual* Vice Chancellor of his Lodge with the same, in an *official* sense *only*, for the purpose of *receiving, examining* and *imparting* the same in the manner with which invested therewith. (*Jour. 1874, 970.*)

300. The Form of a traveling shield, prescribed in 1874, with its provisions, prescriptions, limitations and specifications, as thereon, therein and thereto appended, set forth and expressed, was adopted for use and immediate issuance, and the proper officers were instructed to have the same printed according to the specifications accompanying, and issued *at once*, according to and in the form prescribed. (*Jour. 1874, 970.*)

301. No Knight is permitted to visit any Subordinate Lodge outside of his own Grand Jurisdiction unless in possession of an unexpired traveling shield. (*Jour. 1874, 970.*)

302. Imprint seals and signatures, by the Supreme and Grand Keepers of Records and Seal, on the traveling shield, are by said legislation of 1874 made legal. (*Jour. 1874, 970.*)

(COPY OF FACE OF SHIELD.)

The Supreme Lodge Knights of
{ Seal of Supreme Lodge } Pythias of the World, through the Grand Lodge of the Jurisdiction of ——, authorizes —— Lodge, No. —, of said Jurisdiction, to issue this { Seal of Grand Lodge }

Sig. of S. K. of R. & S.   TRAVELING SHIELD   Sig. of G. K. of R. & S.

To Brother ——, who has attained in the Order the Third, Chivalric, or Knight's Rank. This Shield entitles the bearer to all rights, benefits, privileges and fraternal courtesies of the Order; of entrance into the Castle Hall of any regularly and legally constituted Subordinate Lodge of the Order of Knights of Pythias, when presenting this Shield, accompanied by the A. S. W., and proving himself in the work of the Order. The bearer (whose proper signature appears written on the margin hereof) is entitled to be in possession (or invested with by any C. C. or other proper officer) of the A. S. W. for and during the terms covered by or period for which issued. This Shield is issued for the space of —— months, ending on the —— day of ——, A.D. 18—, P.P. —, and no longer.

All dues must be paid in advance at time when issuing a Shield, and no Shield shall be issued to lap any new year or A. S. W., unless dues for that whole year are paid in advance, nor be used in any sense whatever as a Withdrawal Card. Every visitation or investment of A. S. W. shall be recorded on the back of this Shield by the K. of R. and S. or C. C. of the Lodge when visiting.

{ Seal of }
{ Subordinate } In witness whereof we have appended
{ Lodge } our names and affixed the Seal of our
Lodge, this —— day of ——, in the year
of our Lord one thousand eight hundred
and ——.   —— ——, C. C.
, K. of R. and S.   (*Jour. 1874, 970.*)

(COPY OF BACK OF SHIELD.)

The Constitution and By-Laws of —— Lodge, No. —,
K. of P. of Grand Jurisdiction of ——, allows for weekly
benefits the sum of —— dollars per week, and for funeral
benefits the sum of —— dollars, and this evidences that
Brother Knight —— as a member of this Lodge is entitled
to the same.   —— ——, K. of R. & S.

VISITATIONS MADE.

NAME OF LODGE.	NO.	CITY OR TOWN OF	DAY OF MONTH.	YEAR.	SIGNATURE OF K. OF R. & S.

INVESTED WITH A. S. W.

NAME OF LODGE.	NO.	CITY OR TOWN OF	DAY OF MONTH.	YEAR.	SIGNATURE OF K. OF R. & S.

TRAVELING SHIELD. KNIGHTS. Issued the —— day of ——, A.D. 18—, P.P. — for the space of —— Months, to Brother Knight —— —— Lodge, No. —, of —— of Grand Jurisdiction of —— Expires —— day of ——, A.D. 18—, P.P. —, K. of R. & S.

303. Specifications.—The form of shield to be printed on its face, where issued to those of the Knight rank, in *blue* ink. Those issued to members having received the Past Chancellor's rank to be printed in *green* ink, and add after the word "rank," and before the words "This shield," the following: "and has received the rank of and been enrolled on the roster of the Grand Lodge of this Grand Jurisdiction, according to its Journal, as a Past Chancellor;" and those issued to members having received the Past Grand Chancellor's rank, the same, with this additional: Insert after the words "according to" the word "the" in place of the word "its," and "Journals" instead of "Journal," of that Grand and the Supreme Lodge as a Past Grand Chancellor; the face of this grade of shield to be printed in *red* ink.

Classification of colors of imprint seals, where used, to be as follows:

On shields printed in *blue:* Supreme seal, *red;* Grand seal, *green;* Subordinate seal, *black.*

On shields printed in *green:* Supreme seal, *red;* Grand seal, *blue;* Subordinate seal, *black.*

On shields printed in *red:* Supreme seal, *purple;* Grand seal, *green;* Subordinate seal, *black.* (*Jour. 1874, 971–2.*)

304. The use of the color black for Subordinate Lodge seals being found inconvenient, the Supreme Chancellor in 1874 issued an order that all Subordinate Lodges, not having the imprint seal, might use the impressing seal, without the color (black), in the appropriate place, on all "Traveling Shields" issued by them, and that the same should be recognized as official. (*Jour. 1875, 1018.*)

305. In 1875 the legislation relative to shields passed at the session of Supreme Lodge in 1874 was so amended as to authorize Subordinate Lodges to issue traveling shields to applicants for any length of time from one month to the date of the next meeting of the Supreme Lodge, but no longer; and the dues to be paid by the applicant were required to be paid for the length of time covered by the shield; and thereafter said traveling shield was only to be regarded as evidence of the good standing of the holder in his Lodge, and as a letter of credit or relief shield; and the Supreme Chancellor and Supreme K. of R. and S. were empowered to change the form of the shield in accordance therewith as soon after the adjournment of the Supreme Lodge as possible; and the Supreme Chancellor was authorized to issue a universal S. A. P. W. July 1, 1875, which, in connection with the usual evidence of good standing, should be sufficient to admit any brother into any Lodge of the Order. *(Jour. 1875, 1145; 1876, 1197.)*

In referring to this legislation (Jour. 1876, 1197), in his circular relating thereto, the Supreme Chancellor said: "This password, as its name indicates, will be changed semi-annually, July 1 and January 1 of each year. When the Lodge is open it must be given at the outer door before entering, and must be taken up by the M. at A. on examination at the opening of a Lodge. In view of the legislation referred to herein, the shield is no longer required to enable a member of the Order to visit in or out of his own jurisdiction, the S. A. P. W. being universal. The shield will be issued in a new form, as a relief shield, and should be held by every member as evidence of good standing, and indicating the amount of weekly and funeral benefits to which the holder is entitled. *and in no case should any money be paid unless the shield is presented to any Lodge except his own.* In case of sudden and severe sickness or death among strangers, the relief shield will be a sure evidence of membership, and enlist the aid and sympathy of every true Knight." *(Jour. 1876, 1197.)*

A member holding a withdrawal card is not entitled to a traveling shield or the A. S. W. *(Jour. 1875, 1042, 1114.)*

SIR KNIGHT.
[See Rank and Titles.]

SUBORDINATE LODGES AND THEIR OFFICERS.

1. Composition and institution of.
2. Under control of Supreme Lodge.
3. Name.
4. Meetings and fines for non-attendance.
5. Quorum, order of business, etc.
6. Officers and their duties.
7. Surrender of books and papers.
8. Addressing the Chair.

[See, also, Charters and Dispensations; Constitutions; Membership; Offenses; Uniform, etc., and Condition of Admission, under Uniform.]

(1) COMPOSITION AND INSTITUTION OF.

306. A Subordinate Lodge shall never consist of less than seven members of the Knight rank. [Obligatory.] *Const., Art. viii, Sec. 2.)*

307. At the institution of Lodges the parties must be initiated, proved and charged, the officers elected and installed, their dispensation delivered to the proper executive officer, after which they can receive applications and perform the work usual to a Lodge, but *not* before. It is *not* necessary that *all* the applicants — or in fact any of them — should be members prior to making such application, but it is far better that there should be one or more who have the ranks before so doing. This decision applies only to Lodges under the control of the Supreme Lodge, as each Grand Lodge regulates its own territory in this respect. A party cannot be a member of two Lodges at one and the same time. (*Jour. 1873, App. 37.*)

308. Any member of the Order desiring to assist in the formation of a new Lodge, and signing an application for such purpose, must, upon the institution of such Lodge, present his withdrawal card from his Lodge. (*Jour. 1870, 225.*)

309. Citizens have the right to petition for the establishment of a Lodge of the Knights of Pythias in a place where the Order is already established, provided the application has the approval and sanction of the Deputy Grand Chancellor or officer having charge of the territory where occurring, indorsed thereon. As to whether this may be done in opposition to the wishes of the Lodge or Lodges in active working order, or at least without the recommendation of an established Lodge, it is held that where there is a Grand Lodge in existence, it would be a matter for local legislation; there being none, and the Supreme Lodge having the jurisdiction, it is the duty of the Deputy Grand Chancellor to receive and forward all applications made to him for the institution of new Lodges, and he must approve or disapprove thereof, in writing, of the same, he, the Deputy Grand Chancellor, having no right or authority to arrange with or agree to any side stipulations in the premises, and any Lodge or Lodges objecting thereto must file their objections in writing over their seal with the Deputy Grand Chancellor, which authenticated objection, alleging reasons therefor, must be forwarded by the Deputy Grand Chancellor to this office for final passing on the issue raised. (*Jour. 1873, App. 39.*)

(2) Under Control of Supreme Lodge.

310. All Subordinate Lodges in jurisdictions where no Grand Lodge exists, shall be under the immediate control of this Supreme Lodge until the formation of a Grand Lodge for that jurisdiction, and shall pay to the Supreme Lodge, while under its control, fifty cents per capita tax on each member annually. (*Const., Art. vi, Sec. 1.*)

311. The Supreme Lodge cannot constitutionally (under Art. I, Sec. 4, [old] S. L. Const., (and the rule is probably the same under the new Const.) confer upon a State Grand Jurisdiction authority to grant dispensations or charters for the organization of Subordinate Lodges in other States and Territories; said Lodges to be under the immediate supervision or control of said Grand Jurisdiction until such time as there shall be five Subordinate Lodges instituted in each of said States or Territories, and all revenues whatsoever now derived by the Supreme Lodge in the institution and control of Subordinate Lodges, to appertain to and be transmitted to the Supreme Lodge as soon as received. (*Jour. 1871, 427; 1872, 621, 627.*)

[See new Const., Art. vi, Sec. 1, *supra.*]

312. Until a Grand Lodge is started and regularly instituted, the territory within its jurisdiction belongs exclusively to the Supreme Lodge. (*Jour. 1873, App. 6.*)

313. And Lodges instituted in such territory under the authority of the Grand Lodge of an adjoining State are illegal. (*Jour. 1873, App. 6, 7.*)

314. A Lodge instituted under such circumstances is *irregular*, not clandestine. (*Jour. 1873, App. 8.*)

(3) Name.

315. State Jurisdictions are prohibited from naming Lodges after living persons. (*Jour. 1869, 95.*)

(4) Meetings and Fines for Non-attendance.
[See Delinquent and Defunct Lodges.]

316. A Subordinate Lodge shall hold stated meetings at least once a week, at such an hour as may from time to time be determined upon; *Provided*, that each Grand Lodge may allow meeting at longer intervals by a regular dispensation. [Obligatory.] (*Const., Art. viii, Sec. 2.*)

317. **The questions** whether or not a Grand Lodge has the power to authorize a Subordinate Lodge in its jurisdiction to meet semi-monthly, until the privilege is taken away from it, and whether or not a Grand Chancellor has this power, present matters for local legislation, and are not proper for determination by the Supreme Lodge. (*Jour. 1876, 1284, 1300.*)

318. **The question** as to how many failures of a Subordinate Lodge to hold stated meetings will cause a surrender of charter, is a matter entirely for local legislation, and does not pertain to the Supreme Lodge. (*Jour. 1876, 1285, 1299.*)

319. **On appeal** of P. C. W. R. C. against the decision of the Grand Lodge of Tennessee, in 1875, it appeared that C. was assessed a fine for non-attendance at a regular meeting of a Subordinate Lodge, which fine he refused to pay, on the ground that he was neither an elected nor appointed officer. This decision was affirmed by the Grand Lodge, which held that by a strict construction of the Constitution, a Chancellor Commander, by virtue of his election, necessarily becomes the acting Past Chancellor, and by this is a sitting officer of the Lodge, and liable to fines for non-attendance the same as other officers, and on appeal to the Supreme Lodge this decision was affirmed. (*Jour. 1876, 1306.*)

(5) Quorum, Order of Business, etc.

320. **Not less** than seven members of the Knight rank shall constitute a quorum for the transaction of business, including one qualified to preside; and if seven members only be present, no appropriation of money shall be made unless it be by unanimous consent. [Obligatory.] *Const., Art. viii, Sec. 2.*)

321. **The Lodge** shall transact all its business in the Knight rank, except the actual conferring of the Page or Esquire rank. [Obligatory.] (*Const., Art. viii, Sec. 2.*)

322. **An official order** from the Supreme Lodge or Grand Lodge to any Subordinate Lodge of the Order, and in the order as here given, takes precedence over *all* other business, and when notified of its being there — unless while working one of the sections of a rank, and should such be the case the Lodge must be brought to its proper working rank — the contents made known and acted upon *at once* prior to proceeding with any other business. Should the order be irregular, exceptional or even arbitrary, the after-course will be to obey it until remedied through the proper channels. (*Jour. 1873, App. 35.*)

(6) OFFICERS AND THEIR DUTIES.

[See Ritual.]

323. The officers of a Subordinate Lodge shall be as provided in the Ritual of the Order. [Obligatory.] (*Const., Art. viii, Sec. 2.*)

PAST CHANCELLOR.

(See Grand Lodge; Withdrawal Cards; Vacancies.)

324. The Past Chancellor's degree, being a ritualistic degree, and fully provided for in the Grand Lodge Rituals, can only be conferred in the Grand Lodge, with its attendant ceremonies. It is, therefore, not proper or competent for a Grand Lodge or the Grand Chancellor to direct that, after the admission and instruction of new Past Chancellors at the opening of the session, all Past Chancellors who may afterward present themselves for instruction be obligated and instructed in the ante-room by the Grand Ven. Patriarch. (*Jour. 1874, 913, 935.*)

325. The question of making certain Subordinate Lodge officers Past Chancellors after a certain term of official service is purely a local matter, and not proper to be considered by the Supreme Lodge. (*Jour. 1873, 721; 1875, 1140.*)

326. The question of conferring the degree of Past Chancellor, for eminent services to the Order, is to be determined by the Grand Lodge jurisdictions. (*Jour. 1873, 704, 735; 1875, 1156.*)

327. The question whether, if any Subordinate Lodge shall reëlect a Chancellor Commander, or elect a Past Chancellor to the position of Chancellor Commander, the Lodge shall elect from the floor one Knight as Past Chancellor, on whom the degree of Past Chancellor shall be conferred by the Grand Lodge of the jurisdiction, is a matter entirely under the control of each Grand Jurisdiction. (*Jour. 1873, 699, 734.*)

While this seems to have been always the principle, it would appear to be entirely changed by a literal interpretation of the next paragraph, which contains the action of the Committee on Appeals and Grievances on a case coming from California, where the Grand Lodge, evidently acting on the principle here laid down, declared the right of any Lodge, on reëlecting (misprinted in the Journal "selecting") a Chancellor Commander should have the right to elect one of their numbers upon whom the degree of Past Chancellor should be conferred. This action was reversed, and the decision made as appearing in the next paragraph.

328. Subordinate Lodges have not the right to elect a Past Chancellor, said power belonging to the Grand Lodge. (*Jour. 1874, 927.*)

329. A brother having served a term as Chancellor Commander, at the installation of his successor is *entitled* to the degree, but is not a Past Chancellor in full until he has been obligated and instructed; though it seems there is no good reason why he may not wear a Past Chancellor's regalia in his own Lodge during the interim between the time of service and the Grand Lodge session. (*Jour. 1872, 468, 613; 1874, 845.*)

330. At the institution of a Subordinate Lodge, working under the immediate supervision of the Supreme Lodge, the P. C., C. C., V. C., P., K. of R. S., M. of F., and M. of E., take the rank of Past Chancellor, provided they serve till the end of their official term. After this the rank is obtained only by service as Chancellor Commander. (*Jour. 1875, 1114.*)

331. A Chancellor Commander who is elected for another term is entitled to the Past Chancellor's rank in his Grand Lodge, also the sitting Past Chancellor of a Lodge; *Provided*, that said Chancellor Commander elect shall be installed for his second term. (*Jour. 1875, 1042, 1114.*)

332. The question whether it is competent for a Grand Lodge to confer the rank of Past Chancellor on a retiring Chancellor Commander who has not served a full term as Past Chancellor, is a matter exclusively within the jurisdiction of Grand Lodges. (*Jour. 1874, 940, 944.*)

333. If a sitting Past Chancellor take a withdrawal card from his Lodge, his rank when he deposits his card, would be the rank of Past Chancellor, and he must receive with his card a rank credential as Past Chancellor, and will be entitled to the Grand Lodge rank. (*Jour. 1875, 1043, 1114.*)

334. The status of officiating Past Chancellors and

questions as to whether a sitting Past Chancellor can decline serving in his official position while a member of the Lodge, and so situated that he could serve if he would; whether he can be suspended from serving in that office for inefficiency or neglect to attend to the duties of the office; whether he can resign as sitting Past Chancellor; how, in case of a vacancy from any cause, the office shall be filled; whether he is an officer of the Lodge; whether, when the by-laws of a Lodge impose a fine on all officers of the Lodge absent from the meetings of the Lodge, or require a removal from office if absent three or four consecutive meetings, said penalties can be applied to the sitting Past Chancellor; are proper subjects for local legislation; *Provided*, that no one but a Past Chancellor can be directly elected to fill the position, in case of a vacancy for any cause occurring in said position. (*Jour. 1876, 1234, 1302.*)

CHANCELLOR COMMANDER, AND OTHER SUBORDINATE OFFICERS.

335. Lodges *may* elect whom they please Chancellor Commander, if eligible otherwise under the *local* law. There is no *general* law " making it rotative from lower offices up." (*Jour. 1873, App. 37.*)

336. On appeal of W. L. S. *vs.* The Grand Lodge of Maryland, the gist of the subject was as follows: The appellant claimed the honors of a Past Chancellor, because Meacham Lodge, No. 33, elected to the Chancellor Commander's chair one who had not served a term in the chair of the Vice Chancellor. At the time of the origin of this case the Grand Lodge of Maryland did not require said qualification — said law being approved by the Supreme Body. *Held*, that the action of the Grand Lodge of Maryland should be sustained. (*Jour. 1874, 939.*)

337. Any member who has served in any elective or appointive office is eligible to the office of Vice Chancellor. (*Jour. 1875, 1033, 1134.*)

338. In 1872 a change or amendment in Ritual, where the duties of Keeper of Records and Seal are defined in obligation when installed into office, was made so as to make it the duty of the Master of Finance to notify members who are in arrears for dues, etc., and Keeper of Records and Seal's duty to sign all orders drawn on the banks. (*Jour. 1872, 464, 598.*)

339. The Outer Guard has no right to refuse to inform a brother (applying for admission) what degree his Lodge is at labor in, if such information be asked for at the outer door. It is his duty to state what degree the Lodge is working in, that no errors may occur in giving the signs, etc. (*Jour. 1873, App. 38.*)

340. No person but the Outer Guard is allowed in the ante-room at the opening of a Lodge. (*Jour. 1870, 229.*)

(7) SURRENDER OF BOOKS AND PAPERS.

341. When, by a vote of any Grand Lodge, the Grand Chancellor or any other member is authorized to demand the surrender of any books, papers, or other effects of a Subordinate Lodge, and any officer or member, officers or members, shall refuse to deliver the same, he or they shall forever be excluded from membership if the said Subordinate Lodge should be reinstated, or such a demand be subsequently rescinded by a Grand Lodge. (*Jour. 1869, 90, 94.*)

(8) ADDRESSING THE CHAIR.

342. Any officer or other member retiring from the Lodge under an order from the Chancellor Commander, or entering it again after having performed the duty for which being sent out of the Lodge, is not required to give the sign on retiring or reëntering, but must work his way through the doors. (*Jour. 1873, App. 38.*)

SUPPLIES.

1. By-Laws concerning.
2. How paid for.

[See, also, Revenue; Supreme K. of R. and S. (in Supreme Lodge); Journal of Proceedings.]

(1) BY-LAWS CONCERNING.

343. All printed or other materials furnished by the Supreme Lodge to any Grand or Subordinate Lodge, members thereof, or other parties, for creating a revenue for the Supreme Lodge, shall be known under the general heading of "Supplies;" which said supplies shall be furnished as may be from time to time specified, changed, altered or amended by legislation at the regular sessions, but which for the time being shall be as follows, to wit:

SUPPLIES TO GRAND LODGES.

Dispensation Fee to Grand Lodges $30 00
Charter Fee.. 20 00
Charter Plates for Subordinates 2 00
Grand Lodge Rituals, $5 each, per set of 5......... 25 00
Rituals for Subordinate Lodges, each.............. 2 00
Installation Books for Subordinate Lodges, each.... 40
Odes for Subordinate Lodges, each 5
Odes for Grand Lodges, each 10
Bound Journals of Proceedings of Supreme Lodge,
 in paper....................................... 1 00
Compiled Proceedings of Supreme Lodge, in leather 5 00
Odes of the Order, set to music, per book......... 20
Dedication Ceremonies, per book $1 each, per set... 5 00
Traveling Shields (now Relief Shields) 20
Withdrawal Cards 25

SUPPLIES TO SUBORDINATE LODGES UNDER THE IMMEDIATE JURISDICTION OF THE SUPREME LODGE.

Dispensation Fee...............................$15 00
Rituals, per set of 5 .... 20 00
Installation, per set of 5.......................... 3 00
Odes, 10 cents each, per set of 50................. 5 00
Bound Journals of Supreme Lodge Proceedings, in
 paper 1 00
Compiled Proceedings, in leather................. 5 00
Odes of the Order, set to Music, 40 cents per book;
 per set of 5 .... 2 00
Traveling Shields 40
Withdrawal Cards 50

By reference to the Constitution, Art. I, clauses 1 and 2 of Section 1, it will be seen that these supplies. *their printing and publication*, are "regulated and controlled" by the Supreme Lodge, they being sources of revenue.

OFFICIAL JEWELS FOR SUPREME, GRAND AND SUBORDINATE LODGES, PAST OFFICERS AND KNIGHTS.

Grand Lodge Jewels.

No. 1. Set of 11 Jewels, including two for Supreme
 Representatives.........................$40 00

No. 1. Triangle, German silver, heavily plated with silver. Oval of oreide, heavily gilt and neatly engraved.

No. 2. Set of 11 Jewels $55 00
Triangle and Emblems, coin silver, solid. Shield and oval of oreide, very heavily gilt. More elaborate engraving and chased.

Subordinate Lodge Jewels.

No. 3. Set of 14 Jewels, including four for attendants $18 00
Triangle and White Emblems, of German silver, well silver-plated, neatly engraved and burnished on front. Colored Emblems, of gilt.

No. 4. Set of 14 Jewels $25 00
Triangle and White Emblems, of German silver, triple plated, burnished both sides, more elaborate engraving. Colored Emblems, solid, heavily gilt and chased.

No. 5. Set of 14 Jewels $45 00
Triangle and White Emblems, of coin silver, burnished both sides, very elaborate engraving. Colored Emblems, solid, very heavily gilt and chased.

Past Chancellors' Jewels, Separate from Sets.

No. 6. Same quality as No. 3. Price ....$1 80 each.
No. 7. "   " No. 4. " .... 2 80 "
No. 8. "   " No. 5. " .... 5 00 "

Past Grand Chancellor's and District Deputy Grand Chancellor's Jewels.

No. 9. Same quality as No. 1. Price ....$4 50 each.
No. 10. "   " No. 2. " .... 5 50 "

Knight's Jewels.

No. 11. Same quality as No. 3. Price ....$2 20 each.
No. 12. "   " No. 4. " .... 3 25 "
No. 13. "   " No. 5. " .... 5 00 "

If ten or more Knights' Jewels are ordered at one time, 10 per cent will be deducted from above prices.

All Jewels will have a neat pin, from which the Jewel will be pendant.

MEMORIAL CHARTS.
Form A — Knight's Chart.

Black and tinted border, lettering in center, blue. $1 50 each.
In lots of 100 or more........................ 80 "
    "   75............................. 85 "
    "   50............................. 90 "
    "   25............................. 95 "
    "   10............................. 1 00 "
Less than 10 at one order, at retail price.

Form B — Past Chancellor's Chart.

Black and tint'd border, lettering in center, green $1 75 each.
In lots of 50 or more........................ 90 "
    "   25............................. 95 "
    "   10............................. 1 00 "
    "   5............................. 1 10 "
Less than 5 at one order, at retail price.

Form C — Past Grand Chancellor's Chart.

Black and tinted border, lettering in center, red. $2 00 each.
In lots of 20 or more........................ 1 00 "
    "   10............................. 1 10 "
    "   5............................. 1 25 "
Less than 5 at one order, at retail price.

(By-Laws S. L., printed in Const. S. L. 1876, 22, et seq.)

(2) HOW PAID FOR.

344. In 1871 (*Jour. 410*) the Supreme Lodge adopted a resolution that the Supreme Scribe be strictly forbidden to deliver any supplies to Grand Scribes or others unless the cash accompanied the order asking for such supplies. In 1873 (*Jour. 770*) the Supreme Lodge adopted the following resolution:

"*Resolved*, That the Supreme Recording and Corresponding Scribe be and he is hereby authorized to issue certificates of indebtedness of this Supreme Body for mileage and per diem to its officers and representatives, which shall be accepted in payment for their respective amounts for supplies and representative tax whenever due from the different jurisdictions. On a question arising which legislation should be obeyed, the Supreme Chancellor at a time of great financial embarrassment of the Supreme Lodge, when the effect of enforcing the latter resolution would have been to cut off the only source of revenue to the Supreme Lodge, ruled that the former should be obeyed, and his action was approved by the Supreme Lodge." (*Jour. 1874, 926.* For further action on the subject of these resolutions, see *Jour. 1874, 929, 940.*)

SUPREME LODGE AND ITS OFFICERS.

[See Condition of Admission, under Uniform; Rules of Order.]

1. Powers of Supreme Lodge.
2. How constituted.
3. Sessions.
4. Quorum.
5. The head of the Order.
6. Members: their admission, rights, duties, etc.
7. Credentials.
8. Officers. (a) *Eligibility;* (b) *P. S. C.;* (c) *S. C.;* (d) *D. S. C.;* (e) *S. V. C;* (f) *S. P.;* (g) *S. M. of E.;* (h) *Supreme K. of R. and S.;* (i) *S. M. at A., and I. and O. G.;* (j) *Supreme Lecturer.*

(1) POWERS OF SUPREME LODGE.

345. **The Supreme Lodge** is the source of all true and legitimate authority in the Order of Knights of Pythias wheresoever established; it possesses original and exclusive jurisdiction and power:

1. To establish, regulate and control the Forms, Ceremonies, Written and Unwritten Work, and to change, alter and annul the same, and to provide for the safe keeping and uniform teaching and dissemination of the same.

2. To provide, print and furnish all Rituals, Forms, Ceremonies, Cards and Odes, Charts and Certificates.

3. To prescribe the form, material and color of all Regalia, Emblems, Jewels and Charts, and to designate the uniform of the Order.

4. To provide for the emanation and distribution of all Passwords, and regulate the mode and manner of using the same, and generally to prescribe such regulations as may be necessary to secure the safe and easy intercourse and identification of the brethren.

5. To establish the Order in States, Districts, Territories,

8

Provinces or Countries where the same has not been in-grafted.

6. To provide a revenue for the Supreme Lodge by means of a representative tax on each Grand Lodge and charges for supplies furnished by it, and dues from Subordinate Lodges under its immediate jurisdiction.

7. To provide for annual returns from each Grand Lodge, and for semi-annual returns from each Subordinate Lodge under its immediate jurisdiction.

8. To hear and determine all appeals from Grand and Subordinate Lodges, when the same are properly brought before it in accordance with the regulations of the Order, and to provide by legislation for the enforcement of its decisions.

9. To enact laws and regulations of general application to carry into effect the foregoing and all other powers reserved by this Constitution to the Supreme Lodge or its officers, and such as may be necessary to enforce its legitimate authority over Grand and Subordinate Lodges under its immediate jurisdiction.

10. To charter Grand Lodges and to define the territorial extent of their jurisdiction, and to charter Subordinate Lodges not within the territorial jurisdiction of any Grand Lodge, and to provide a Constitution for each Subordinate Lodge under its immediate jurisdiction.
(*Const., Art. i, Sec. 1.*)

(2) How Constituted.

346. The Supreme Lodge shall consist of:
1. All Past Supreme Chancellors.
2. Past Supreme Chancellor.
3. Supreme Chancellor (presiding officer).
4. Supreme Vice Chancellor.
5. Supreme Prelate.
6. Supreme Master of Exchequer.
7. Supreme Keeper of Records and Seal.
8. Supreme Master-at-Arms.
9. Supreme Inner Guard.
10. Supreme Outer Guard.
11. Two Supreme Representatives from each Grand Lodge under the jurisdiction of the Supreme Lodge, until there are 20,000 members belonging to one Grand Lodge;

and one Supreme Representative for each additional 10,000 members; *Provided*, that no Grand Lodge shall be entitled to more than four Supreme Representatives. (*Const., Art. ii, Sec. 1.*)

(3) SESSIONS.

347. Sessions of the Supreme Lodge shall be held annually, at such time in the months of April, May, June, July or August, as the Supreme Lodge may at each annual session determine; *Provided*, that if the Supreme Lodge neglects to fix any special time it shall convene on the third Tuesday of April. (*Const., Art. iv.*)

The Act of Incorporation also states "that the said Supreme Lodge *shall* hold an Annual Session at such time and place as a majority of its members *present* may determine." Associating the words in Art. IV, "at each Annual Session." and the words "members present," quoted from the Act, we had supposed that this was the only legal process by which the Annual Session could be convened and the business legally transacted; but it appears that though at the session of 1876 it was "*Resolved*, that the next session of this Supreme Lodge be held on the fourth Tuesday of August. 1877, commencing at 10 o'clock A.M.," yet that the Supreme Officers, in view of certain circumstances, as set forth in the following circular, considered it competent to accept the *written consent* of the Representatives, though not in session, and on said consent changed the day appointed and ordered at the previous Annual Session under the constitutional provision and Act of Incorporation. (*Jour. 1876, 1332.*)

To the following circular I received replies unanimously in favor of changing the time of meeting to the *third Tuesday of August, 1877:*

CORUMBUS, OHIO, October 3, 1876, and P. F. XIII.

To the Officers and Representatives of the Supreme Lodge, August Session, 1876:

Since your adjournment, I have learned that the Grand Encampment of Knights Templar of the United States hold their Triennial Session at Cleveland, on the fourth Tuesday of August, 1877. That is the time fixed by you for the next session of the Supreme Lodge. In view of the fact that the Grand Encampment named its time at the last session held in New Orleans, in 1874, and that there will be several thousand in attendance thereat, it is thought best to change the time of the meeting of the Supreme Lodge to the third Tuesday of August, 1877, in order that ample accommodation may be had at the hotels of Cleveland. The Supreme Chancellor joins with me in asking your approval of the change of time of meeting; and a prompt answer is desired, so that the change can be made in the printed Journal.

Fraternally.   JOSEPH DOWDALL, *S. K. of R. & S.*

348. The place for the holding of each annual session shall be fixed at the preceding annual session; *Provided*, that if no place is fixed by the Supreme Lodge, the annual

session shall be held in the city of Baltimore. (*Const.,
Art. iv.*)

Though according to Art. III, Sec. 2, among the special prerogatives
of the Supreme Chancellor, it states that he can "call special sessions of
the Supreme Lodge," yet it does not anywhere designate the manner of
the call or the business which can be transacted at such a session. In the
Articles of Incorporation, however, in section 6, it would appear that he is
clothed with certain powers *outside* the Constitution, and shall, if it be
the rule, "on the call of the Supreme Representatives of ten (10) Grand
Jurisdictions in writing, convene an extra session of said Supreme Lodge
at Washington City, D.C."

(4) Quorum of Votes.

349. A majority of the Grand Lodges shall constitute a
quorum to transact business. (*Const., Art. ix.*)

(5) The Head of the Order.

350. As at present constituted, the Supreme Lodge
is in fact what its name not only imports, but expresses, viz.,
the only Head of the Order in the World; and as a conse-
quence, no organization, Lodge or other collection of men,
claiming or pretending to act as a Lodge of Knights of
Pythias, save and except under and by virtue of the authority of this "Head of the Order," can be, or have any right
to claim to be, any part of the organization. (*Jour. 1875,
1141.*)

(6) Members: their Admission, Rights, Duties, etc.

351. New members are only admitted to the Supreme
Lodge at the opening of the morning sessions of the two
first days and the morning session of the last day. (*Jour.
1875, 1166.*)

352. A member of a Grand Lodge whose returns for
the year and Supreme Representative tax have not been
regularly and annually forwarded to the proper Supreme
Officers on or before the 1st day of May prior to any session
of the Supreme Lodge, shall in no case be entitled to a vote,
either by being an Officer or Supreme Representative.
(*Const., Art. ix; Jour. 1871, 410, 426.*)

353. The proper construction of Articles IX and
XVIII of Supreme Lodge Constitution is, that by the failure to do the act before described in said article, a delinquent Grand Lodge *forfeits its right* to representation in
the Supreme Lodge, but the Supreme Lodge *may,* by spe-

cial vote, *permit* as a *privilege* (but not as a *right*) the said
Grand Lodge, through its representatives, to be heard on
the floor of the Supreme Lodge. (*Jour. 1875, 1160, 1164.*)

[See Returns.]

354. **Members of the Supreme Lodge** named in the
preamble to a resolution as having been guilty of disre-
garding the Supreme Lodge legislation have no right to
vote thereon. (*Jour. 1870, 219.*)

355. **All Past Grand Chancellors** duly recognized by
the Supreme Lodge shall be admitted to its session and be
entitled to seats therein, but shall not be entitled to speak
unless by permission of the Supreme Lodge, and shall not
be entitled to vote. (*Const., Art. ii, Sec. 3.*)

356. **One who has only served** as Vice-Grand Chancellor of a Grand Lodge, not having been elected to the
degree of Past Grand Chancellor, and such Grand Lodge
having been organized since the next preceding session of
the Supreme Lodge, is not entitled to a seat in the Supreme
Lodge as a Past Grand Chancellor. (*Jour. 1872, 446.*)

357. **Where** at the January session, 1873, of the Grand
Lodge of Pennsylvania W. J. M. was duly elected to the
office of Grand Chancellor, to serve for the term of *one year*,
or, in other words, until the annual session to be held in
January, 1874, and was regularly installed into said office,
and entered upon the discharge of its duties; and at the
semi-annual session of the Grand Lodge, held in July, 1873,
a new Constitution for the Grand Lodge and Subordinate
Lodges was adopted, and went into force on the 26th of
September, 1873; and at the said session of the Grand
Lodge (July, 1873,) a resolution was adopted (see G. L.
Journal of July, 1873, 535,) that in the event of the approval and promulgation of the new Grand Lodge Constitution, before the 1st of January, 1874, the present Grand
Lodge Officers, Representatives and District Deputy Grand
Chancellors be continued in their several positions until
the third Tuesday of August, 1874; and by Article II of the
new Grand Lodge Constitution the annual session was
fixed for the third Tuesday of August, and the semi-annual
session for the third Tuesday of February in each year; and
at the semi-annual session of February, 1874, charges were
preferred against the Grand Chancellor, and a resolution

adopted ordering him to vacate his position as Grand Chancellor until the annual session in August, and directing the Vice-Grand Chancellor to act as Grand Chancellor until that time was passed; and at the annual session in August, 1874, a resolution was adopted by said Grand Lodge that said W. J. M. be deprived of his certificate as Past Grand Chancellor, and be suspended for three years (see Proc. G. L. Penn., 1874, 149, 150); on a question arising as to the validity of the credentials, the status and rights of P. G. C. W. J. M. as an applicant for admission as a member of-the Supreme Lodge: *Held*, that although service is the base of honor in this Order, and although he having served the full term, as expressed in the law at the time of his election, would be, and *prima-facie* was, entitled to admission, yet this did not hinder or prevent the Supreme Lodge from barring its portals against the entrance of an improper person, or from excluding from admission such an one for matters arising after the issuing of the certificate; and that, without passing upon the guilt or innocence of W. J. M., his certificate having been withdrawn by the Grand Lodge, and he never having been introduced to the Supreme Lodge, and instructed in the Supreme Lodge rank, he was not entitled to admission as a member of the Supreme Lodge. (*Jour. 1875, 1127-1129.*)

358. Supreme Representatives must be Past Grand Chancellors in good standing in their respective Grand and Subordinate Lodges, and shall be elected as follows: At the next annual election after the adoption of this Constitution, and annually thereafter, each Grand Jurisdiction shall elect, in the mode provided for electing Grand Lodge Officers in the Constitution of the respective Grand Lodges, one Supreme Representative to serve for two years: *Provided*, that each Supreme Representative now admitted shall continue in office to the expiration of his present term. In case of the vacancy in the office of the Supreme Representative, from death, removal or any other cause, the Grand Lodge which he represented shall determine how such vacancy shall be filled. At the organization of any new Grand Lodge two Supreme Representatives shall be elected, one to serve for one year and one to serve for two years; *and provided further*, where any Grand Jurisdiction is entitled, under the provisions of this Constitution, to more than two Supreme Representatives, the additional representative or representatives shall be elected biannually, in conformity to this Constitution, and in such a manner that if there are four representatives the terms of two thereof shall expire each alternate year. Each Officer and Supreme Representative shall be entitled to one vote in determining any question before the Supreme Lodge, and each Past Supreme Chancellor shall be entitled to discuss any question, but not to vote. (*Const., Art. ii, Sec. 2.*)

359. **A Grand Chancellor** who is not already a Past Grand Chancellor, is not eligible to the office of Supreme Representative, if elected before his successor is installed. (*Jour. 1874, 908; see this rule explained in Jour. 1875, 1034.*)

On appeal against the action of the Grand Lodge of New York, the facts material to the question were as follows:

Article VI, Section 1, of the Constitution of the Grand Lodge K. of P. of the State of New York, reads as follows: "The elective officers of this Grand Lodge shall be Grand Chancellor, Grand Vice Chancellor, Grand Scribe, Grand Banker and two Representatives to the Supreme Lodge." At its annual session held at Brooklyn, in 1875, P. G. C. J. H. M. was elected Supreme Representative to the Supreme Lodge immediately after his successor, G. C. F. P. H. was installed Grand Chancellor of the Grand Lodge of New York. This action of the Grand Lodge of New York was claimed by the appellant to be illegal, and it was sought to have his seat declared vacant. *Held*, that J. H. M., who came with proper credentials of his membership, a certificate of his regular election, signed by the Grand Chancellor, attested by the Grand Keeper of Records and Seal, and having the seal of the Grand Lodge of New York attached, was, under the resolution found on page 1113, Jour. of 1875,— "that hereafter any Grand Chancellor who has served a full term in that office, and against whom no charges are pending, shall be entitled to the rank and title of Past Grand Chancellor as soon as his successor is installed,"—entitled to a seat as a member. (*Jour. 1876, 1266.*)

360. **One** who has served but a term as Vice-Grand Chancellor is not eligible to the position of Past Grand Chancellor, and cannot be a Supreme Representative. (*Jour. 1872, 537.*)

361. One not a member in good standing of a Subordinate Lodge cannot be a Supreme Representative. (*Jour. 1872, 444.*)

362. There is no law of the Order authorizing the election of alternate Supreme Representatives. (*Jour. 1871, 342, 343.*)

363. Where a State, entitled to only three Supreme Representatives, elected four, the representative receiving the lowest number of votes at the time of his election was declared not entitled to a seat in the Supreme Lodge. (*Jour. 1876, 1276, 1318.*)

364. The appointment of Supreme Representatives by a Grand Chancellor is not in accordance with the law of the Supreme Lodge, unless the Grand Lodge has conferred said power upon the Grand Chancellor. (*Jour. 1872, 443.*)

365. But Sec. 3, Art. VI, Const. of G. L. of New York, as follows —"The Grand Chancellor shall preside at all sessions of the Grand Lodge; enforce order and decorum; decide all questions of order without debate, subject, however, to an appeal to the Grand Lodge by two members; *appoint Grand Officers pro tem. in case of the temporary absence or disqualification of any Grand Officer;* appoint all committees, unless otherwise ordered,"— is a sufficient authority for the Grand Chancellor to appoint Supreme Representatives. (*Jour. 1872, 444.*)

Query. As under Art. III, Sec. 6, and Art. VII, Sec. 5. of the new Constitution, Supreme Representatives are not Grand Officers (though probably intended to be), would this ruling hold?

366. Where a Grand Lodge declared the office of its Supreme Representative vacant, on the ground that he had never taken his seat in the Supreme Lodge, and named another in his stead, the latter was admitted by the Supreme Lodge to a seat therein. (*Jour. 1869, 64–66.*)

367. In future, the functions of the office of a Representative shall cease at the call to order of the Supreme Lodge by the Supreme Chancellor, or his deputy or successor, at the biannual sessions, and the newly-elected Representatives admitted, whose credentials have been passed upon, and they shall be entitled to all the pecuniary benefits arising thereby as Representatives. (*Jour. 1870, 198.*)

(7) CREDENTIALS.

368. For an instance, where a telegraphic dispatch from the Grand Chancellor of a State, appointing a Supreme Representative in the place of one who had resigned, was accepted as sufficient credentials. (*See Jour. 1875, 1095, 1096.*)

369. It is the duty of the several Grand Keeper of Records and Seals to forward the certificates of the Grand Representatives and Past Grand Chancellors to the Supreme Keeper of Records and Seals at least twenty days before the session of the Supreme Lodge. (*Jour. 1871, 410.*)

(8) SUPREME LODGE OFFICERS: (*a*) ELIGIBILITY.

370. No one shall be eligible to any office in the Supreme Lodge unless he has been duly admitted to the Supreme Lodge, by being either a Representative or a Past Grand Chancellor. (*Const., Art. ii, Sec. 4.*)

(*b*) PAST SUPREME CHANCELLOR.

371. The Past Supreme Chancellor shall have charge of and supervise the arrangement of the Altar, or any other necessary floor-work. (*Const., Art. iii, Sec. 1.*)

372. The retiring Supreme Chancellor fills the chair of S. V. P. (now Past Supreme Chancellor.) (*Jour. 1870, 194.*)

(*c*) SUPREME CHANCELLOR.

373. The Supreme Chancellor shall exercise, as occasion may require, all the rights appertaining to his high office, in accordance with the usages of the Order. He shall have a watchful supervision over all Lodges, Grand and Subordinate, and see that all the constitutional enactments, rules and edicts of the Supreme Lodge are duly and promptly observed, and that the dress, work and discipline of the Order everywhere are uniform.

Among his special prerogatives are the following:

To call special sessions of the Supreme Lodge, or conventions of Supreme Officers in council.

To visit any Grand or Subordinate Lodge under the immediate jurisdiction of this Supreme Lodge, and to give such instructions and directions as the good of the Order may require, always adhering to the obligatory usages of the Order; to cause to be executed and securely to pre-serve and keep the official bonds and securities of the Supreme Master of Exchequer and Supreme Keeper of Records and Seal.

To grant warrants of dispensation during the recess of the Supreme Lodge for the institution of new Subordinate Lodges, which dispensations to be in force until taken up by charters granted in lieu thereof by a properly instituted Grand Lodge, and to promptly notify the Supreme Keeper of Records and Seal of the issuing of said warrants of dispensation.

To grant warrants of dispensation during the recess of the Supreme Lodge for the institution of Grand Lodges in States, Countries, Districts, or Territories where the same have not been established.

To manage the contingent fund of the Supreme Lodge, and suspend or remove any derelict or contumacious officer for *cause*, he having right to appeal to the Supreme Lodge; and to fill any vacancy by appointment until filled by regular election.

To appoint and commission a *Deputy Supreme Chancellor* for special purposes of instituting Grand Lodges and installing their officers, or otherwise, as may be required, in all States, Districts, Territories or Countries where Lodges are established, and not having any Grand Lodge. He shall at the next regular session present a full report of his acts during the recess of the Supreme Lodge. He may hear and decide such questions of law as may be submitted to him by Grand and Subordinate Lodges under the immediate jurisdiction of this Supreme Lodge, and all such decisions shall be binding upon the bodies submitting the same until fully passed upon and disaffirmed or reversed by this Supreme Lodge. (*Const., Art. iii, Sec. 2.*)

374. It is a prerogative of the Supreme Chancellor to confer the degrees of the Order upon candidates *at sight*, after being satisfied that the applicant is qualified according to law. (*Jour. 1869, 69, 108, 118.*)

The resolution on page 118 was, that our present Supreme Chancellor be empowered to make Knights at sight for the advancement of this Order, and that he be permitted the use of any Lodge room for this purpose during the sessions of the Lodge. The prerogative is, however, stated in general terms on page 108. And there does not appear to have been any legislation divesting " the Supreme Chancellor of the Supreme

Lodge of the Order of the Knights of Pythias" of that prerogative which was *exercised for two full terms.*

375. The necessary expenses incident to traveling to any point and back to original starting point, for the purpose of instituting any Subordinate or Grand Lodge by the Supreme Chancellor or his deputy, shall be paid by the Lodges instituted. (*Const., Art. xxiii.*)

[See Jour. 1873, 737, 753.]

(*d*) DEPUTY SUPREME CHANCELLOR.
[See Honors.]

376. All Past Grand or Past Chancellors of *full* rank regularly authorized and commissioned by the Supreme Chancellor to institute Grand Lodges, or to travel under his instructions to exemplify the Work, shall be known, commissioned and styled Deputy Supreme Chancellors. (*Const., Art. xxii.*)

377. All Deputy Supreme Chancellors (of jurisdictions in which there are no Grand Lodges) shall install the officers of all Subordinate Lodges within their jurisdictions, or cause the same to be done, and perform such other duties as the Supreme Chancellor may direct. (*Const., Art. iii, Sec. 8.*)

378. The appointment of Deputy Supreme Chancellor requires no approval by the Supreme Lodge. (*Jour. 1875, 1153.*)

379. The Deputy Grand Chancellor (under old Constitution, corresponding to Deputy Supreme Chancellor of the new Constitution), being the representative of, *in fact*, the Supreme Chancellor, his appointee, created by his selection and authority, necessarily owes his official existence (subject to removal at will or pleasure, and thoroughly under the control of the Supreme Chancellor, who is personally liable for the Deputy Grand Chancellor's actions) to no one but the officer vesting him with the rights and prerogatives of that office. (*Jour. 1873, 719, 746; App. 13.*)

The following is the form of commission adopted for Deputy Supreme Chancellor:

OFFICE OF THE SUPREME CHANCELLOR OF THE SUPREME
LODGE KNIGHTS OF PYTHIAS OF THE WORLD,

———, ———, A.D. 18—.

To all to whom these presents may come, GREETING:

KNOW YE, That having especial trust and confidence in

our Knightly Brother in "F. C. B.," —— ——, who, having attained the high, honorable and responsible rank of Past Chancellor in this Chivalric Order, now belonging to and on the Roster of —— Lodge, No. —, of ——, and who is the bearer of this our Credential,

That we do Appoint, Authorize, and Commission him, the said Past Chancellor, —— —— our Deputy, with the Rank and Grade of Deputy Grand Chancellor, for, and over, the —— of —— or otherwise, as by me directed, where his official duties for or during the term ending April 17, A.D. 18—, may require, unless sooner vacated by the institution of a Grand Lodge, in regular form, and under the laws of the Supreme Lodge Knights of Pythias of the World; said Deputy Grand Chancellor to act according to and under my instructions as the Supreme Chancellor of, and the Constitutions, Laws, Usages, Ceremonials and Formulas, as established, and governing the Supreme Lodge Knights of Pythias of the World, and Lodges appendant thereto and under its control, or until revoked by me as said Supreme Chancellor, prior to the expiration of hereinbefore mentioned term.

This Commission may be Revoked, Annulled, or Taken Away, at the pleasure of the Supreme Chancellor.   In witness whereof we have hereunto affixed our Official Seal and Sign Manual, the day and year above written, and of the Pythian Period the ——   —— ——,

{ S. C.'s }
{ OFFICIAL }
{ SEAL }

Supreme Chancellor K. of P. of the World.
(*Jour. 1873, 719, 746; App. 12.*)

380. Under the old Constitution it was held that a Deputy Grand Chancellor had no authority to grant a dispensation to organize a Lodge.   (*Jour. 1868, 26, 45, 47.*)

(e) SUPREME VICE CHANCELLOR.

381. The Supreme Vice Chancellor, in the event of the death, removal or physical incompetency of his superior, shall act as Supreme Chancellor; at all other times he shall perform such duties as may be assigned him by the Supreme Lodge or the Supreme Chancellor. (*Const., Art. iii, Sec. 3.*)

(f) SUPREME PRELATE.

382. The Supreme Prelate shall open and close the

Supreme Lodge with prayer, and perform all obligatory ceremonial as prescribed in the Ritual or usages of the Order, and such other duties as comport with his office. (*Const., Art. iii, Sec. 4.*)

(*g*) SUPREME MASTER OF EXCHEQUER.
[See Committee.]

383. The Supreme Master of Exchequer shall render to the Supreme Chancellor a quarterly statement of the condition of funds in his hands, and make to the Supreme Lodge at its regular sessions a true and perfect account of his doings, together with an account of all moneys received and disbursed, giving items in detail — the earnings thereon accrued from interest or other investments; to pay all orders drawn on him by the Supreme Chancellor, properly attested by the Supreme Keeper of Records and Seal. For the faithful performance of his duties he shall give bond, to be executed and approved before his installation, in the sum of ten thousand dollars, with unexceptionable securities, or otherwise the office to be declared vacant, and filled by election. (*Const., Art. iii, Sec. 5.*)

(*h*) SUPREME KEEPER OF RECORDS AND SEAL.
[See Committee.]

384. The Supreme K. of R. and S. shall keep a just and true record of all the proceedings of the Supreme Council and Lodge at each session, and transmit annually to each Grand Lodge as many copies thereof as the Lodge has Past Grand Chancellors and officers, and one copy for each Subordinate Lodge in their several jurisdictions, and one to each Lodge under the immediate jurisdiction of the Supreme Lodge. He shall collect all the revenues of the Supreme Lodge, and pay over the amount to the Supreme Master of Exchequer whenever it reaches the sum of $100. He shall also preserve the archives, have charge of the seal, books, papers and other properties of the Supreme Lodge, and deliver the same to his successor when required so to do by the Supreme Lodge. He shall prepare all charters for Grand Lodges; notify officially all Grand Lodges and officers and members of the Supreme Lodge of all sessions of the Supreme Lodge; carry on the necessary correspondence of the Lodge; keep a register which shall contain a list of all dispensations and charters granted to Grand, or warrants of dispensation issued by the Supreme Chancellor for Subordinate Lodges, and a record of all Past Grand Chancellors and Representatives entitled to seats in the Supreme Lodge. He shall attest all necessary official papers and documents, perform such other duties as are required by the laws and regulations of the Order, and as the Supreme Chancellor or Supreme Lodge may from time to time direct. He shall be furnished with an office, and shall have regular office hours, and give notice to all Grand Lodges of the time at which he will so attend, and at each session present a report of the general condition of the Order to the Supreme Lodge. He shall have power to provide himself, at the expense of the Supreme Lodge, with such books, papers and stationery as are necessary for the fulfillment of his duties, and keep in his office a copy of the seal of each Grand and Subordinate Lodge. He shall submit a quarterly trial balance to the Supreme Chancellor for examination, as also render to each regular session of the Supreme Lodge full and exhaustive copies of his accounts with the Grand and Subordinate Lodges, etc., of and during the whole term of recess passed. He shall receive for his services the sum of $1,000 per annum, payable quarterly. For the faithful performance of his duties he shall give bond, to be executed and approved before his installation, in the sum of $10,000, with unexceptionable securities, or otherwise the office to be declared vacant, and filled by election. (*Const. Art. iii, Sec. 6.*)

In 1872 it was enacted that thereafter the appropriation for stationery, expenses, etc., of the department of the Supreme Scribe be paid by the Supreme Banker upon the drafts of the Supreme Scribe, countersigned by the Supreme Chancellor, and that a detailed and vouched account of the expenditures of such appropriation be annually submitted by the Supreme Scribe to the Supreme Lodge. (*Jour. 1872, 633, 637.*)

This was under the old Constitution. *Query*, whether it is now applicable.

385. It is made the duty of the Supreme K. of R. and S. to submit in detail his annual report of supplies ordered and received, in the same manner as the report on printing, etc., submitted by him at the second annual session of the Supreme Lodge (page 172 printed Journal), and that he also report in detail at each annual session such supplies belonging to the Supreme Lodge as he may have on hand. (*Jour. 1872, 624; 1874, 987.*)

386. It is made a part of the duty of the Supreme. K. of R. and S. to take charge of the Supreme Lodge Officers' regalia. (*Jour. 1869, 121.*)

387. It is the duty of the Supreme K. of R. and S. to carefully preserve all printed Journals of Proceedings, and all periodicals of the Order received by him, and at all suitable times cause the same to be bound in permanent binding for preservation in the archives of the Order. (*Jour. 1876, 1275.*)

388. A Board of Auditors, with full powers to audit and examine the books and accounts of the Supreme R. and C. S. and Supreme Banker, and to adopt such measures as may appear best for the investigation of the financial affairs of the Supreme Lodge, has [under the old Constitution] been held to be out of order and unconstitutional. (*Jour. 1873, 681, 729.*)

(i) SUPREME MASTER-AT-ARMS, AND INNER AND OUTER GUARDS.

389. The duties of the Supreme Master-at-Arms, Inner and Outer Guards, are such as are traditionally appropriate to their respective stations, or such as may be assigned them by the Supreme Lodge. (*Const., Art. iii, Sec. 7.*)

(j) SUPREME LECTURER.

390. The matter of appointing a Supreme Lecturer to visit and instruct all Lodges desiring instruction in the Secret Work, is a matter for local jurisdiction. (*Jour. 1873, 694, 734.*)

SUPREME REPRESENTATIVES.
[See Supreme Lodge; Terms.]

SUSPENSION.
[See Benefits. Dues.]

TACTICS.

1. *Adopted.*
2. *Uniform Division.*

(1) ADOPTED.

391. At the session of 1872 the Supreme Lodge

adopted a system of tactics for the use of the Order, recommended by the Grand Lodge of the District of Columbia, and in the same form as presented, with the addition of the following:

G. C., or his deputy, shall rank as Chief Commander.

V. G. C., or his deputy, shall rank as First Assistant Chief Commander.

G. R. and C. S., or his deputy, shall rank as Second Assistant Chief Commander.

G. B., or his deputy, shall rank as Third Assistant Chief Commander.

G. G., or his deputy, shall rank as Chief Executive.

G. I. S., or his deputy, shall rank as Quartermaster.

G. O. S., or his deputy, shall rank as Aid-de-Camp.

W. C. C., or his deputy, shall rank as Chief of Division.

W. V. C., or his deputy, shall rank as First Assistant Chief of Division.

W. R. S., or his deputy, shall rank as Second Assistant Chief of Division.

W. F. S., or his deputy, shall rank as Third Assistant Chief of Division.

W. B., W. G., W. I. S., W. O. S., or their deputies, shall rank as four Guides as Sub-Chiefs.

Attendants, four Assistant Guides. (*Jour. 1872, 602.*)

This system has since been recognized as official. (*Jour. 1875, 1136.*)

392. The Supreme Lodge having adopted a "Manual of Tactics," no other can be used. (*Jour. 1875, 1041, 1115.*)

This was by decision of the Supreme Chancellor, and the committee to whom it was referred reported a resolution approving it, but recommending a committee to examine and modify the "Manual of Tactics" theretofore adopted, and report at the next session. When the report of the committee came up for consideration, it was resolved that a committee of three be appointed, to examine and report at the next session, a Manual of Drill for the use of the Knights of Pythias, which committee has not yet reported (Jour. 1876, 1331); but no direct action seems to have been taken upon the decision itself, which, not being reversed, seems to be the law. (*Jour. 1875, 1045.*)

(2) UNIFORM DIVISION.

393. The laws of the Order contain no constitutional provision warranting the formation of such an organization as a "Uniform Division, Knights of Pythias." (*Jour. 1876, 1315.*)

TERMS.

394. A **term** of the Supreme Lodge shall be two years, and the term of Subordinate Lodges, working immediately under the control of the Supreme Lodges, shall be six months, and the terms of Grand Lodges shall be one year, and that the terms of Subordinate Lodges, working under the control of Grand Lodges, shall be remitted to the several Grand Jurisdictions; *Provided*, that no term of a Subordinate Lodge shall be less than six months. (*Const., Art. xxxii, adopted in 1876, Jour. 1328, 1331.*)

[See Jour. 1875, 1030, 1113, 1136; 1876, 1228, 1229.]

395. The **term** of Supreme Representative is the calendar year, that is to say, from the 1st day of January to the 31st day of December of each year. (*Jour. 1876, 1296.*)

TRUSTEES.
[See Board of Trustees; Incorporation.]

UNIFORM, REGALIA, ETC.

1. Constitutional provisions: (a) *Subject regulated by Supreme Lodge;* (b) *full regalia;* (c) *regalia of Supreme Lodge;* (d) *condition of admission;* (e) *regalia of Grand Lodges;* (f) *regalia of Subordinate Lodges.*
  2. Outside regalia or uniform; specifications.
  3. Emblems of Official rank.
  4. Funeral rosette.
  5. Apron.
  6. Jewels: Official and Past Official, and Knight's.
  7. Miscellaneous decisions.

[See, also, Committees; Supreme Lodge; Supreme Keeper of Records and Seal.]

(1) CONSTITUTIONAL PROVISIONS: (*a*) SUBJECT REGULATED BY THE SUPREME LODGE.

The regulation of regalia of the Order ought not to be introduced into a Grand Lodge Constitution, as any change made in regalia by the Supreme Lodge might cause a conflict between the two laws. (*Jour. 1876, 1309.*)

396. The **regalia** of the Supreme, Grand and Subordinate Lodges shall be such as is prescribed by the Supreme Lodge, or adopted and approved from time to time

9

at the regular sessions of the Supreme Lodge. (*Const.,
Art. xii.*)

(b) FULL REGALIA.

397. All Supreme, Grand or Subordinate Lodge Officers appearing in the prescribed uniform of the Order indicative of their rank, and wearing the proper and prescribed
official Jewel on their left breast; or,

All Past Supreme, Grand or Subordinate Lodge Officers
appearing appareled in a like manner, wearing the proper
and prescribed Past Official Jewel on their left breast; or,

Any and all Knights appearing and appareled in a like
manner, with the Knight's Jewel on his left breast, shall be
considered in full and complete regalia for all Lodge conventions, meetings or session purposes, being entitled to
admission to and seat within any Lodge of the Order (if
otherwise qualified and entitled to admission) wherever existing. But in the absence of the uniform, the Jewel alone
shall not be considered sufficient regalia, except for officers
of Subordinate Lodges in their conventions and at their
stations; and the following shall be the regalia, when used,
of the several bodies as below, to wit:

(c) REGALIA OF SUPREME LODGE.

398. The regalia of the Supreme Lodge shall be as
follows (see old regalia described in Jour. 1868, 39):

For Past Supreme Chancellor.—A purple collar, skirted
with scarlet and white, the scarlet to be inside; to be
trimmed with helmet, globe and tassels, lace and fringe of
gilt bullion. Jewel, of white and yellow metals, to be worn
pendant thereto, with the words " Past Supreme Chancellor "
enameled or engraved on the border.

For Supreme Chancellor and Supreme Vice Chancellor.—
Collars of purple, skirted with scarlet, of the same form,
style and trimming (including helmet and globe) as the
sitting Past Supreme Chancellor. Jewels to be of yellow
and white metals, as provided and adopted, of the same
device in emblems, unless otherwise specifically stated, as
those worn by the corresponding officers of Grand and Subordinate Lodges, and to be worn suspended from the collar,
in the same manner as above stated, or used in prescribed
manner for them.

For remaining Supreme Officers.—Same as specified for Supreme Chancellor.

For Supreme Prelate.—White collar, skirted with scarlet, trimmed with gilt lace and bullion fringe and tassels. On the right breast of the collar shall be embroidered in gilt bullion a visored helmet, with ax and lance crossed, illustrative of the name and general character of the Order. On the left breast shall be embroidered in gilt bullion a globe, emblematical of universal fraternity, and the Supreme authority of this Lodge. The Jewel, of white and yellow metals, shall be as prescribed and adopted, to be worn suspended from the collar where the ends are united, or suspended on the left breast in open sight, if in uniform, and detached from regalia.

For Supreme Representatives.—The same as Past Grand Chancellor's, with "S. R." upon the right-hand side of collar, in gilt bullion, with Jewel pendant, or as otherwise prescribed for members in uniform. (*Const., Art. xxx.*)

(*d*) CONDITION OF ADMISSION.

399. No Past Officer, Representative or member shall be allowed to enter the Supreme Lodge when in session, unless properly uniformed and jeweled, or clothed in the established regalia of his rank, according to these prescriptions, with Jewel appended thereto: *Provided*, any Past Chancellor, officer, or member presenting himself at the door of any Lodge of the Order properly uniformed, as prescribed by the Supreme Lodge law, with the Past Official, Official, or Knight's Jewel on his left breast, in open sight, shall be recognized as in proper regalia, and be entitled to admittance, if otherwise qualified. (*Const., Art. xxx.*)

It would seem by this clause that, in amending Article XXX in 1876, this portion was lost sight of, as, by reference to the subsequent paragraph herein, under "Regalia of Subordinate Lodges" (see "*f*" of this article), it will be seen that the "proper uniform" as required above is not now considered requisite. *Query*, Which governs?

(*e*) REGALIA OF GRAND LODGES.

400. The working regalia of Grand Lodges shall be as follows, to wit:

For Past Grand Chancellors.—Black velvet collar, trimmed with gold lace and fringe, and "P. G. C." embroidered in gold on left side, with the approved and adopted Jewel pendant.

For Past Chancellors.—Red velvet collar, trimmed with gold fringe, and adopted and approved Jewel pendant.

[See Jour. 1870, 213.]

For Representatives.— Same as Past Chancellors, rosette with number of Lodge on left side, and approved and adopted Jewel pendant. Said rosette to be furnished by the Subordinate Lodge represented.

For Officers.— Same as Past Chancellors, with the prescribed insignia of office of their rank, adopted and approved Jewel pendant: *Provided*, any Officer, Representative or Past Chancellor presenting himself properly uniformed as prescribed by the Supreme Lodge law, with the Past Official or Official Jewel on his left breast, in open sight, shall be recognized as in proper regalia, and be entitled to admittance, if otherwise qualified. (*Const., Art. xxx.*)

(*f*) REGALIA OF SUBORDINATE LODGES.

401. The working regalia of Subordinate Lodges shall be as follows, to wit:

For Pages, a blue collar; for *Esquires,* a yellow collar; for *Knights,* a red collar. *Officers' Regalia.*—For C. C., a collar of scarlet velvet, with silver fringe one and a half inches long, and silver lace border on inner edge half inch wide, with Jewel pendant; for V. C., the same as the C. C., with Jewel pendant; for Prelate, a black velvet collar, trimmed same as C. C. and V. C., with Jewel pendant; for M. of E., the same as the V. C., omitting the fringe, with Jewel pendant; for M. of F., the same as the M. of E., with Jewel pendant; for K. of R. and S., the same as the M. of F., with Jewel pendant; for M. at A., the same as the K. of R. and S., with Jewel pendant; for I. G., the same as the M. at A., with Jewel pendant; for O. G., the same as the I. G., with Jewel pendant; for P. C., the same as the C. C., with gold fringe, with Jewel pendant; or, in other words, plain collars, the same as the above in every particular, *except* the embroidered emblems as heretofore used, and in their place the adopted metal Jewels hanging pendant thereto: *Provided*, that any and all Lodges of this Order, whereever hereafter started, on and after July 1, 1874, shall procure and use only the plain regalia and prescribed metal

Jewels (if desiring both), or Jewels alone; that any and all Lodges now having and using the regalia *with* the "embroidered emblems" *on* them, may do so until worn out, but when replacing them, either in part or whole, shall conform strictly to the provisions as herein expressed and above set forth; conditioned that no part of this provision shall be so construed by any authority to prevent Lodge Officers, when working, using the Jewels alone, without any regalia, or any Lodge now having and using the style of regalia with embroidered emblems thereon, from using the metal Jewel in connection therewith: *Provided*, any Past Chancellor, officer or member presenting himself properly uniformed as prescribed by the Supreme Lodge law, with the Past Official, Official, or Knight's Jewel on his left breast, in open sight, shall be recognized as in proper regalia, and be entitled to admittance, if otherwise qualified: *Provided, however*, any Past Supreme Officer, Supreme Officer, Supreme Representative, Past Supreme Representative, Past Grand Officer, Grand Officer, Past Chancellor and Subordinate Lodge Officer, and Knight wearing the Jewel of his rank on the left lapel of the coat in a Lodge, shall be considered in full regalia. (*Const., Art. xxx.*)

(2) Outside Regalia or Uniform; Specifications.

402. At the session of 1871 a uniform regalia, described below, was recommended for use where practicable or desirable, subject to the final adoption of the different Grand Lodges of the various jurisdictions as controlled by their own action and legislation, or proper official orders. (*Jour. 1871, 362, 396, 409.*)

403. At the session of 1872 it was enacted that all portions of the uniform or outside regalia, as established by the action of the Supreme Body at its session held in Philadelphia, A.D. 1871, except helmet, oriflamme, gorget and cloak, be declared in its present shape and detail the permanent uniform or outside regalia for the use of the Order, and which shall not be changed, mutilated or reduced, in any sense of substitution, for the space and term of *ten* years from the date of that session. (*Jour. 1872, 630; 1876, 1319.*)

404. The detailed specifications of such outside re-

galia or uniform costume for the order are found in Jour.
1872, 486, *et seq.*, and are as follows:

FULL GALA AND INSPECTION DRESS.

Coat, pants, sword, belt, baldric, cloak, gorget, gauntlet
cuffs, gloves, helmet and oriflamme (with fatigue cap, covered, hung to sword belt).

ORDINARY PARADE DRESS.

Coat, pants, sword, belt, baldric, gauntlet cuffs, gloves, helmet and oriflamme (with fatigue cap, covered, suspended
from belt).

FATIGUE DRESS.

Coat, pants, sword, belt, fatigue cap (uncovered) and white
gloves.

COAT.

Black cloth, cut military style, single-breasted, standing
collar (with a half roll to the sixth button from the bottom),
nine buttons in front, two behind, length to knee, side
edges plain, hook and eye at neck gorge, seam plain, two
buttons at cuff, buttons flat black silk lasting.

PANTALOONS.

Black cloth or doeskin cassimere, and of uniform style.

CLOAK.

A half-cloak—a *cavalier*—or cape of appropriate material, make and color, emblazoned thereon, embroidered
on proper colored cloth or velvet, the crest of the Order,
to be worn over the left shoulder and back, fastened by a
cord and tassel of appropriate color. The "gorget" worn
with the same made of *three* triangular points, one of which
will be *scarlet*, one *sky-blue* and one *orange*. Pendant to the
point of each proper color will be the appropriate letter in
solid white metal. The *gorget* to be separate, and fastened
on by buttoning under collar of cape or by cord and tassel.

*For Members and Subordinate Officers (inclusive of Worthy
Chancellor).*—Cloak *dark blue*, crest *scarlet*.

*For Past Chancellors and Grand Officers (of less rank than
Grand Chancellor).*—Cloak *orange*, crest *blue*.

For Grand and Past Grand Chancellors.—Cloak *scarlet*,
crest *blue*.

For Supreme and Past Supreme Chancellors.—Cloak *purple*, crest *gold*.

HELMET.

The metal helmet adopted in 1871 is described as follows:

White metal, of lightest possible durable construction,
regulation shape, wide scales and feather socket at the top,
triangular in shape, with *point* of triangle to the front.

In 1875 a helmet of a different description was adopted,
described as follows:

Black body, in shape (like sample); round top, rim in
front and flowing back; front visor two inches and rear
visor two and a half inches in length; black cone, running
from tip of back to center front; cone, two and a half
inches high in front, running back to point at tip of flowing
back; raised wire for plume support, from back tip to front
of cone, one-half inch above cone.

Gold (or silver) cord, double, and looped from center
sides to front, fastened at sides with helmet-shaped button.

Escutcheon on front as follows:

For Knights: Shield-shaped escutcheon, one and a half
inches.

For Past Chancellors (of less rank than Grand Chancellor): Triangle-shaped escutcheon, two inches from tip to
tip.

For Grand Chancellor and Past Grand Chancellor: Oval-
shaped escutcheon, two inches in shortest diameter.

For Supreme Officers and Past Supreme Officers: Circular-shaped escutcheon, two inches in diameter. (*Jour.
1875, 1159.*)

Those who, prior to the adoption of the above, had procured the metal helmets (described above) are allowed to
wear them. (*Jour. 1875, 1159.*)

DISTINCTIONS.

Knights and Past Chancellors (of less rank than Grand
Chancellor) will wear white metal or silver; Grand Chancellors and Past Grand Chancellors will wear yellow metal
or gold. (*Jour. 1875, 1159.*)

PLUME.

The plume adopted in 1871 was also changed in 1875
(see Jour. 1875, 1159) as follows:

In shape an oriflamme, running from back of cone to
front, and drooping over front, to be worn as follows:

For Knights.—Red.

For Past Chancellors.—Blue.

For Grand Lodge Officers.—Yellow.

For Past Grand Chancellors.—Red, tipped (on sides and front) with white.

For Supreme Officers and Past Supreme Officers.—Purple, tipped (on sides and front) with white.

The Plume adopted in 1871 was described as follows:

In shape an oriflamme, of *three* standing feathers, upper end curling to the front, and to be worn according to rank, as follows:

For Pages, *one* "blue" feather on front point of socket.

For Esquires, *one* "blue," *one* "yellow" at rear point of socket.

For Knights and Subordinate Lodge Officers, *one* "red" (at front point of socket), *one* "yellow," *one* "blue" (at rear points of socket).

For Past Chancellors. *three* "blue" feathers.

For Grand Officers, *three* "yellow" feathers.

For Past Grand Chancellors, *three* "red" feathers, *en double* or *echelon*.

For Supreme and Past Supreme Chancellors, *three* "white" feathers. *en triple* or *echelon*.

No reference being made in legislation of 1875 to Pages and Esquires, *query*, whether they have a right to wear a plume.

CAP.

Present navy style, black cloth, three to three and a half inches height of crown; narrow, black leather straps, fastened at sides with shield-shaped buttons. The crest or escutcheon of the Order on the front, and gold or silver lace running around the band of the cap, according to rank of wearer.

ESCUTCHEON AND LACE.

For Knights, Esquires and Pages.— Silver-plated METAL, shield-shaped escutcheon, and 3 LIGNE silver lace.

For Subordinate Officers (inclusive of Worthy Chancellors). Shield-shaped, EMBROIDERED escutcheon, on BLUE velvet and 6 LIGNE silver lace.

For Past Chancellors.—Shield-shaped, EMBROIDERED escutcheon, on GREEN velvet and 6 LIGNE silver lace.

For Grand Officers (inclusive of Grand Chancellors).— Shield-shaped, EMBROIDERED escutcheon, on ORANGE velvet and 9 LIGNE silver lace.

For Past Grand Chancellors.—Oval-shaped, EMBROIDERED escutcheon, on RED velvet and 12 LIGNE gold lace.

For Supreme and Past Supreme Chancellors.— Circular-shaped, EMBROIDERED escutcheon, with vine around, and "S. C." or "P. S. C.," on PURPLE, and 15 LIGNE gold lace.

BALDRIC.

To be worn by all members of less rank than Grand Chancellors. Five inches wide, in the whole, of blue bordered with yellow, one inch on either side; a strip of army lace, one-fourth of an inch wide, at the inner edge of the yellow. On the front center of the baldric, a metal triangle with raised — or struck up — escutcheon of the Order. On center field of the triangle, and on each uncovered point thereof, one of the three letters " F. C. B.," so that the whole three may appear. The baldric to be worn from the right shoulder to the left hip, with ends extending six inches below the point of intersection, under and at the lower edge of the sword belt, and be fastened with shield-shaped white metal screw button, the top of which will overlap the sword belt, and hold the baldric firmly in its place on the right shoulder.

BELT.

Red enameled or patent leather, two inches wide, fastened around the body with white metal clasp of emblematic design; two short, white metal chains suspended from red leather sliding straps on belt, and white metal slide, with hook for fatigue cap.

SWORD.

For all members and officers of less rank than Grand Chancellor. Thirty-four to forty inches long, white metal scabbard, cross-handle black hilt. Helmet head with appropriate devices, suspended by chains from two side-rings. For all Officers and Past Officers, from rank of Grand Chancellor up, same as above, except gilt in place of white metal, and white instead of black grip.

GAUNTLETS.

Black leather, military style; cuff to extend four and a half inches up from its intersection with the hand, and to have a shield-shaped metal escutcheon of the Order (two inches in length) on back of cuff, or, black kid gloves with patent leather cuffs (of proper length and color), separate or together, as most convenient to wearer (and in fatigue dress white gloves WITHOUT the cuffs). Knights, Chancellors and Grand Officers (of less rank than Grand Chancellor), SILVER-plated escutcheons. Grand and Past Grand Chancellors, and Supreme and Past Supreme Chancellors, GOLD-plated escutcheons.

Emblems of Official Rank.

SHOULDER STRAPS FOR OFFICERS.

For Supreme and Past Supreme Chancellors.—Royal purple silk velvet, four inches long by two inches wide, outside measurement, bordered with *three* rows of corded embroidery *in gold*, each one eighth of an inch wide; the escutcheon or crest of the Order at each end, and globe or world in center. The Past Supreme Chancellor's same as Supreme Chancellor's, and to have in addition three small stars in silver, one at the center of top and one each at the right and left corners at the foot of the strap. All other Supreme Officers' same size; color and embroidery as Supreme Chancellor's, with the exception of the escutcheon or crest at the ends, in place of which the initials (in old English characters) of their office, as equally divided as possible, at each end of the strap, *all in gold.*

For Past Grand Chancellors.—Bright red silk velvet, four inches long by two inches wide, with *two* rows of corded embroidery, each one-eighth of an inch wide, and escutcheon or crest of the Order embroidered in the middle *in gold*, and the letters " P.G.C." (in old English characters), embroidered *in silver*, on the lower end of the strap.

For Grand Chancellors.—Bright orange silk velvet, same size and embroidery as Past Grand Chancellor's, except in center is embroidered, *in silver*, a gauntlet closed and grasping the truncheon of office, and at lower end of strap, *in silver* (in old English characters), the letters "G. C."

For all other Grand Officers.—Same size, design, color, shape and embroidery as Grand Chancellor's, except in center of strap a shield (instead of gauntlet, etc.), and at the lower end (in old English characters) the initials of their office, but *all in silver.*

For Past Chancellors.—Bright emerald green silk velvet, three and a half inches long by one and a half inches wide, bordered with one row of embroidery, one-quarter of an inch wide, crossed battle-axes in center, and letters " P. C." (in old English) at lower end, *all in silver.*

For Worthy Chancellor.—Bright blue silk velvet; same size and design as Past Chancellor's in other respects, except in center is embroidered, *in silver*, crossed-swords and a hand-lance *in gold*, running lengthwise of the strap through the swords, head toward the foot, and the letters "W. C." (in old English characters) at the foot of the strap, *in silver.*

For Vice Chancellor.—The same as Worthy Chancellor's, except, instead of crossed-swords in center is simply a tilting lance, running LENGTHWISE, head toward the foot of strap, and letters "W." and "V." in center, on either side of lance, and "C." at foot of the same, covered by head of the lance, *all in silver.*

For other Subordinate Lodge Officers.— Same as Worthy Chancellor's and Vice Chancellor's in color, and embroidery on edges; no design, but with simply the letters (in old English) or initials indicative of the various offices in TRIANGULAR arrangement in the center.

ARMS.

For Pages.— Battle Axe and Shield, of appropriate make and material.

For Esquires.— Lance and Shield, of appropriate make and material.

For Knights.— Sword and Shield, as prescribed, and of appropriate make and material.

For Officers and Past Officers.—Swords, as heretofore prescribed.

DISTINCTIONS.

Pages, Esquires, Knights, Chancellors, Past Chancellors and Grand Officers (of less rank than Grand Chancellor) will wear WHITE METAL or SILVER wherever metal, embroidery or lace appears, unless otherwise specifically stated. Grand and Past Grand Chancellors, Supreme and Past Supreme Officers, YELLOW METAL or GOLD, wherever metal, embroidery or lace appears, unless otherwise specifically stated. (*Jour. 1872, 486–499.*)

See the distinctions adopted in 1875 (Jour. 1875, 1159) in connection with new helmet (*ante*). *Query,* whether the above distinctions are affected thereby, as to Pages, Esquires, etc., which are not therein referred to.

(4) FUNERAL ROSETTE.

405. In 1872 the following was adopted as the new funeral rosette of the Order, which may or shall be worn in lieu of other regalia:

By Knights, Pages and Esquires.—Round rosette, black, flat center, one and a half inches in diameter, with white metal struck up or silver embroidered escutcheon, surrounded by two rows of one-half inch black satin ribbon, the joint made by the ribbon joining the center of the rosette, to be covered with one-quarter ligne silver braid, the completed rosette to be three inches in diameter. Suspended from the under side of the rosette a white silk ribbon, two and a half inches wide and four and a half inches long, with name and number of Lodge, and the letters " K. P." printed upon it in black, the white ribbon to be covered with black crape.

By Past Chancellors.— Same as for members, but guilt escutcheon.

By Officers.— Same as for members, but substituting the emblem of their respective offices for the escutcheon in center of the rosette. (*Jour. 1872, 620, 631.*)

[See Sec. 7, *post.*]

For the legislation upon the old funeral rosette, see Jour. 1869, 99, 116; 1871, 403, 413. This legislation is as follows:

FUNERAL BADGES FOR GRAND LODGES AND SUBORDINATES.

A rosette three inches in diameter, with black velvet center of two inches, with gold letters " G. L." and one-half inch red border (ribbon) to be worn as a badge of mourning by Grand Lodges on the occasion of attending funerals.—*Resolution of Annual Session, 1869.*

Resolved, That the funeral rosette or badge adopted by the Supreme Lodge for Grand Lodges be also adopted for Subordinate Lodges, except that the appropriate colors and emblems for Subordinates shall be used.— *Session of 1871.*

(5) APRON.

406. At the session of 1871 (subsequent to the recommendation of a uniform) it was enacted that any jurisdiction then using the apron regalia be allowed to continue its use as an outside regalia until the Supreme Lodge, by a direct vote through its Supreme Representatives, established an outside regalia. (*Jour. 1871, 411.*)

(6) JEWELS: OFFICIAL AND PAST OFFICIAL, AND KNIGHT'S.

407. At the session of 1874, the designs and specifications for " *Official Jewels* or Emblems for the officers of Supreme, Grand and Subordinate Lodges," were adopted by the Supreme Lodge K. of P. in lieu of those then in use. (*Jour. 1874, 973.*)

SUPREME LODGE OFFICERS' JEWELS.

Design.—An elaborate wreath on a four-inch "Circle," representing the World, and inclosing all below or
appendant to it.

Specifications.— "Circle" to be in Yellow Metal.
"Triangle" " White " where not
"Emblems" " Yellow " [enam'd.

GRAND LODGE OFFICERS' JEWELS.

Design.—A plain three and one-half inch "Oval," inclosing
"Shield," which covers and guards the "Trian-
gle" that constitues, makes and supports it.

Specifications.—"Oval" to be in Yellow Metal.
"Triangle" " " White "
"Shield" " " Yellow "
"Emblem" " " White "

SUBORDINATE LODGE OFFICERS' JEWELS.

Design.—A plain three inch "Triangle," representing the
three fundamental principles of the Order, "F. C.
B." (except P. C. and C. C., as below them).

Specifications.—The basis of all White Metal "Emblems"
on Nos. 1 to 11 inclusive, White Metal,
except the "Escutcheons" on Nos. 1, 2 and
3, and the "Book" on No. 4, which are
Yellow Metal.

Explanatory of No. 1.—The shape of "Jewel" and "Escutcheon" represents the officer
who has passed, and now rests on
his laurels and overlooks the obtuse
and acute "Triangles."

Explanatory of No. 2.—The shape of "Jewel" and "Escutcheon" represents the officer
who governs the whole Lodge.

Explanatory of No. 3.—The shape of "Jewel" and "Escutcheon" represents the officer
who watches and guards one "Triangle."

Explanatory of No. 4.—The shape of "Emblem" on "Jewel," the officer who confers the
moral essence that pervades our
customs and usages, that ought to
be universal as the "Circle" of the
World, whereon the "Book" rests.

408. The "Official and Past Official Jewels" of the Order of K. of P. for any of the grades of rank shall suffice, when worn by the officer or members of proper rank, in connection with or separate, and in lieu of, any other distinguishing marks, as the legal insignia of *that* rank, office, or other position in the Order, that may require or entitle the wearing of the same, and may be worn at the option of said officer or officers, member or members, with or *without* the regalias, as now used — whether official or working; and when worn in either case shall be recognized, acknowledged, obeyed, and carry all legal weight and effect therewith, as heretofore given the regalia or other insignia of any rank of the Order. (*Jour. 1874, 974.*)

409. The embroidering or blazoning of any of the legal Official or Past Official Jewels or designs, on any material whatever, with a view of using the same in *any* sense as working or official regalia of the Order of K. of P., is prohibited, and rendered illegal and void, whenever or wherever introduced, or attempted to be sold or used. (*Jour. 1874, 974.*)

410. These legal Official and Past Official Jewels, as now adopted, shall be made out of "metal," of uniform appearance, finish, size, shape, trimming, and design, for each proper grade as above stated. (*Jour. 1874, 974.*)

411. The legislation of 1874 respecting Official and Past Official Jewels, also settled the details of the method by which they should be furnished to the Order, as follows:

"*Resolved*, That the P. S. C., S. C., and S. K. of R. & S. be and they are hereby authorized and empowered to arrange with some proper and responsible manufacturers to make and create dies or other machinery necessary to their manufacture, on one of the following bases, to wit:

"*First*, The manufacturer to agree upon some fixed *minimum* figure for each set, basing his calculations on *two hundred sets of Jewels;* this *minimum* to cover the cost of and include all dies and machinery required to make and finish the same ready for use; and after the delivery of and receiving the pay for said two hundred sets of Jewels, at said *minimum* price, then said dies and special machinery to become the vested property of this Supreme Lodge, subject to its order, removal and control.

"*Second*, After said two hundred sets of Jewels are made, delivered and paid for, then these hereinbefore mentioned officers and said manufacturer shall again agree and settle on a new *minimum* for all sets of Jewels made thereafter, or if not agreeing they may arrange with other manufacturers, if procuring better terms therefor, and use the same dies and machinery then belonging to this Supreme Lodge; in case said officers fail in the arranging for the foregoing terms, then they may complete arrangements as follows, to wit:

"*First*, Arrange for the manufacturer to make said dies and machinery at his own risk, and to be retained as his own property, and then on a basis of *five hundred sets*, submit his *minimum* figure of cost prices charged therefor; and,

"*Second*, That so soon as the amount of five hundred sets are sold, used or exhausted, then said officers and said manufacturer shall agree and establish a new *minimum* figure for all sets of Jewels made thereafter; and,

"*Third*, That in any and all agreements or contracts perfected, arranged or made by said officers with any manufacturer, shall be so made that no advance payments shall be required of or from them, or this Supreme Lodge, on account of said contract or agreement; that the *minimum* shall be the lowest possible price to be had from responsible parties, and that none shall be manufactured or delivered to any person whatsoever unless upon a *written* or printed order from the Supreme K. of R. and S., and then *only* when paid for by either that officer or the party receiving the same; and,

"*Fourth*, When any agreement, as heretofore mentioned, in either of the modes mentioned, or otherwise, is made, a *positive* reservation shall be made that said manufacturer shall not ask or receive any portion of the price as affixed, as the *maximum* price of same, to be sold for, beyond that properly belonging to them, and as established as the *minimum* cost price; or, if so receiving any excess by "C. O. D.," or other collections, then said excess collected shall be immediately turned over by said manufacturers to the Supreme K. of R. and S., for the use and benefit of this Supreme Lodge; and,

"*Fifth*, That no direct shipments shall be made unless as heretofore set forth and ordered by the Supreme K. of R.

and S., and then *only* when paid for at time of receiving said order, or the same sent " C. O. D." for the *maximum* amounts as fixed and settled on, and then with the expense of packing and return collection added thereto; and be it further

" *Resolved*, That when ascertaining said *minimum* of price, then said officers shall affix a proper *maximum* price thereon, *conditioned*, that in no case shall said maximum yield less than 10 per cent profit, nor exceed 50 per cent profit, after allowing for any incidental expenses or commissions allowed to dealers for the disposing of the same; and be it further

" *Resolved*, That on the said Official and Past Official Jewels being arranged for, and a definite time established for the same being ready for delivery, the Supreme Chancellor and Supreme K. of R. and S. shall promulgate said fact, and solicit Lodges to file their orders accompanied with the established price therefor with the Supreme K. of R. and S. for future delivery." (*Jour. 1874, 974.*)

412. **Any** Jewels used, worn or made by any person or persons whatsoever, differing from those prescribed in 1874, are pronounced illegal in character and unlawful in use, in so far as regards Lodges of the Order of K. of P., and are prohibited for use in any sense whatsoever, unless otherwise legislated for by the Supreme Body, *except* it be the " *embroidered* " *semblance*, as appearing in Art. XI, [old] Subordinate Constitution as made by the Supreme Lodge for the government of all Lodges in this particular, and those *only* when already *embroidered* on the working regalias of Lodges *now* in use. (*Jour. 1874, 975.*)

413. **Any** and *all* Jewels of the Order of K. of P., when used, if *not* coming from or through the Supreme K. of R. and S. of the Supreme Body, and according to and in keeping with the legislation of 1874, are illegal, and prohibited from use by any person or persons, Lodge or Lodges; and the Grand Officers and Deputy Grand Officers are solicited to aid and assist in causing the legal Jewels now adopted being used, and *ordered* to see that *all* others, of whatsoever nature, character, make or kind, unless as set forth in said legislation of 1874, are, if used, *ordered discontinued at once*, under penalty, and that none be permitted used in any way, shape or manner, except those made and procured

under said legislation, and from the proper officers as therein named and set forth. (*Jour. 1875, 975.*)

[See Const. 1874, Art. xxx.]

KNIGHT'S JEWEL.

414. In 1874 the Supreme Lodge adopted and established a badge of the Order, to be recognized and known as the "Knight's Jewel," to be of the form, shape, style, material and design set forth•in design below, with particulars and specifications thereof, and how, when and in what manner the same shall be procured or worn. (*Jour. 1874, 977.*)

415. The said "Knight's Jewel" is manufactured and governed by each and every particular clause, part or provision, in legislation offered, covering and applying to "Official" and "Past Official" Jewels, except where the word or words "set" or "sets" appear, the same is struck out, in so far as applying to the "Knight's Jewel," and the words "each Jewel" inserted in their place. (*Jour. 1874, 977.*)

416. The use of the "Knight's Jewel," or "Past Official" or "Official" Jewel, when occurring in either of the hereafter enumerated cases, *shall* answer in place and fill *all* requirements of the present law as regards working regalia; or as follows, to wit:

1. Any member presenting himself in his own or any sister Lodge of this Order, or at the door thereof, in any one of the "full gala," "ordinary parade," or "fatigue dress" — either with or *without* the sword — as adopted by this Supreme Lodge for the use of the Order at large, and bearing on his left breast, in sight, this "Knight's Jewel," or a "Past Official," or "Official" Jewel, and being *otherwise qualified*, shall be entitled to remain in or be admitted to said Lodge *without his assuming the prescribed* working regalia.

2. Any member who is *not* in either of said classes of uniform cannot legally wear or use said Jewel for any purpose whatsoever, or at any time, and if so worn they are of *no effect or weight whatever;* or, in other words, if in uniform, the Jewel properly worn is sufficient working regalia; if not in uniform, the working regalia *must* be worn in *all* cases, *regardless of the use of a Knight's or other Jewel.* (*Jour. 1874, 977.*)

Under the last paragraph of Art. XXX of the Constitution adopted in 1876, the second clause of this section does not hold, as a member can

10

now claim admission, being otherwise qualified, by wearing the Jewel on the left lapel of his coat.

417. The legislation of 1874 provided that as soon as the "Knight's Jewel," or "Past Official" or "Official" Jewels shall be ready for delivery, or a definite time set for the issuance of the same, as theretofore mentioned, and provided for by reference to the other legislation as referred to, the Supreme Chancellor and Supreme K. of R. and S. shall promulgate such fact to the Order at large, setting forth their uses, benefits and privileges thereto appending, and asking *each* and *every* uniformed member or Past Officer to complete his equipment by ordering and purchasing one for his own use, as also soliciting others to do the same. (*Jour. 1874, 978.*)

418. Design for Knight's Jewel.—A solid Triangle, with an oval Escutcheon of the Order resting thereon, representing that the whole Order rests upon the elemental Triangle of F. C. B.

Size.—Triangle same size, shape, make and material as those prescribed for Subordinate Officers of a less grade of rank than Chancellor Commander. The *oval Escutcheon* to rest on Triangle, be struck up in center, leaving corners plain; and the oval Escutcheon to be made of yellow metal, or enameled in proper emblematic colors. Letters "F. C. B." to be struck up in corners of Triangle, or else be fastened on; if the latter, they also to be in yellow metal, or enameled in proper emblematic colors.

The *back* of the Triangle to bear an impress of a character to denote *its* "official" issuance in proper form; as also place for the name, number and location of Lodge to be engraved thereon of the owner of said Jewel.

The *Escutcheon* or holder of it to be of yellow metal, with pin, or lock for fastening, and Shield on front for engraving name thereon. No Jewel to be complete or legal until fully engraved as herein expressed. (*Jour. 1874, 978.*)

All legislation making it obligatory upon the owner of a Jewel to have his name, number and location of his Lodge engraved thereon, was repealed in 1875. (*Jour. 1875, 1136.*)

Manner of using.— By wearing on the left breast (with coat buttoned), in sight, or on left side coat lapel (if coat is unbuttoned), but always in plain sight.

When to be used.—1. In Lodge rooms when in uniform — with or without sword — and *not* having the proper working regalia on.

2. To gain admission to any Lodge of the Order, when entitled to enter or visit, and otherwise being correct, *if in uniform, without using other* working regalia.

3. At any celebration or parade, *when in uniform;* if *not* in uniform, *their use is prohibited in any way, shape, manner or form.* (*Jour. 1874, 978.*)

[See note to Sec. 416, *ante.*]

How to be procured.—1. From the Supreme Scribe, by regular order for and in your name, and which order *must* be accompanied by the established price in *cash*, or its equivalent, charged therefor. (*Jour. 1874, 978.*)

The second paragraph of this report permitted the procurement of Jewels in a manner other than the above, but was since repealed. (*Jour. 1874, 978; 1875, 1135, 1136.*)

3. Any and *all* officers are charged to see that no illegal or irregular Jewels are permitted to be used; and if *positively known* to be illegal or irregular, it is their duty to PEREMPTORILY challenge their use whenever seen, known or met with. (*Jour. 1874, 979.*)

4. Any "Knight's Jewel" procured from any person or dealer, unless known to be authorized by the Supreme K. of R. and S. to sell and dispose of the same, *are* illegal in every sense of the word, and *must* be challenged by any one cognizant of that fact, at *all* times and places. (*Jour. 1874, 979.*)

419. It was also enacted at that session that the Supreme Chancellor, Supreme Keeper of Records and Seal and Supreme Master of Exchequer be a committee to provide for furnishing and issuing jewels, charts, etc., and they are hereby anthorized to delay the furnishing and issuing of the jewels, memorial charts, etc., authorized at this session, until such time as, in their judgment, the finances of the Supreme Lodge will justify them in doing so, in such quantities and upon terms as will secure profit to the Supreme Lodge. (*Jour. 1874, 989.*)

(6) MISCELLANEOUS DECISIONS.

The decisions prior to the adoption of the new Constitution, while they may not in all respects be binding, are inserted for convenience of reference.

420. A Grand Chancellor and Grand Officers have a right to wear the full fatigue uniform when visiting or instituting a Lodge, but must wear the proper prescribed working regalia. (*Jour. 1872, 627.*)

421. Officers of Lodges *must* wear their official regalia in the Lodge room and while working, regardless of the fact of being in full *outside* "uniform or parade dress." (*Jour. 1872, 615, 627; 1873, App. 36.*)

422. A brother has the right to enter or sit in a Lodge room with a collar suited to his rank and station, being clothed in the uniform regalia as adopted by this Supreme Lodge. (*Jour. 1872, 638.*)

423. Past Officers and Knights wearing the Jewel must always wear a collar or uniform in the Lodge room, as working regalia. The collar may be worn without the Jewel, but the uniform never, in a Lodge room. (*Jour. 1875, 1042, 1114.*)

[See note to Sec. 416, *ante.*]

424. Where the members of a Lodge desire to form a musical band, composed wholly of members of the Order, and to be known as the "Knights' Band," it is not allowable for them to wear the fatigue cap and belt, or any portion of the Knights' uniform, as a band uniform, when on band duty, on occasions not connected with the Order. Brethren are permitted to use the uniform adopted by the Supreme Lodge only when performing the duties requiring its use. (*Jour. 1875, 1154, 1156.*)

425. The uniform cap of the Order, as adopted, shall not be worn in a Lodge room during its sessions, except by order of the Chancellor Commander. (*Jour. 1873, 683, 740.*)

426. The collar cannot be worn in a street parade of any character. Lodges may appear in public parade, at funerals, wearing the funeral rosette on left breast, with or without Jewels; or in plain citizens' dress; also in uniform, with or without Jewels. Except as above, the prescribed uniform, with or without Jewels, must be worn in public parade. (*Jour. 1875, 1032, 1124.*)

427. The matter of prohibiting the practice of Subordinate Lodges appearing in the working regalia of the

Order at picnics, balls, lectures, etc., before the public, pertains to the Grand Jurisdictions. (*Jour. 1872, 619, 628.*)

VACANCIES.

[See. also, Elections ; Supreme Lodge and its Officers ; Resignation.]

428. All vacancies in Subordinate Lodges by death, removal, suspension, resignation or otherwise, shall be filled in the manner of the original selection to serve the residue of the term, and officers so serving shall be entitled to the honors of the term. [Obligatory.] (*Const., Art. viii, Sec. 2.*)

429. Upon the re-election of a Grand Chancellor, and the G. V. P. declines serving the second term, the vacancy must be filled from among the Past Grand Chancellors. (*Jour. 1872, 469, 613.*)

This would now apply to the case of the resignation of a sitting Past Grand Chancellor, and inferentially imply that the Past Grand Chancellor held over with the Grand Chancellor.

430. If the first V. P. resigns, the vacancy is filled by appointment,· and the V. P. serving in that capacity has the honors of the office. (*Jour. 1872, 620, 630.*)

This would now apply to the sitting Past Chancellor.

431. On appeal of J. B. M. from the action of the Grand Lodge of Ohio, in 1874, it appeared that the above Grand Lodge had authority to elect six (6) Past Grand Chancellors, and at the time appointed to elect the above Past Grand Chancellors, P. C. J. B. M. was duly chosen as one of the six Past Grand Chancellors, and the credentials were passed upon by the Supreme Lodge. Some two years after the above election it was claimed and decided by the said Grand Lodge (Ohio) that J. B. M. was not a member of the Order at the time of his election, and by action of the Grand Lodge his election was declared null and void, and a Past Chancellor was chosen in his place. The Grand R. and C. S. issued a withdrawal card to the said P. C. J. B. M., which the Grand Chancellor declined to sign without further enumeration of fact. *Held*, that the credentials of J. B. M. having been passed upon by the Supreme Body, there was no vacancy, and the Grand Lodge had no right to elect one in the place of J. B. M. (*Jour. 1874, 932.*)

VISITATION.

[See Password ; Vouching ; Withdrawal Cards.]

432. Objections cannot be made to a member in good standing and otherwise correct while visiting another Lodge. If anyone is satisfied he is unworthy to sit in a Lodge room, he must proceed against him under our penal laws, or keep silent. (*Jour. 1875, 1042, 1114.*)

VOUCHING.

[See Shields ; Password.]

433. No vouching is allowed in the Order under any circumstances. (*Jour. 1870, 229.*)

WITHDRAWAL CARDS.

1. When granted.
2. Revocation, etc.
3. Renewal.
4. Rank credentials.
5. Carry S. A. P. W. for how long.
6. Cannot be used as visiting cards.
7. In cases of defunct Lodges.
8. Effect of issue in irregular form.

(1) When Granted.

434. Applications for withdrawal cards shall be made, either personally or in writing, to a Lodge, and a card thereupon shall be granted, provided the brother be clear of the books, free from charges made or pending, and there be no other valid objection. [Obligatory.] (*Const., Art. viii, Sec. 2.*)

(2) Revocation, etc.

435. Any withdrawal card may be revoked by a Lodge granting the same, or ordered vacated by the proper Grand Lodge, or Grand Chancellor, at any time, for cause appearing, and when so revoked for the purpose of impeachment or trial, the person holding said card shall again become subject to the Lodge which issued same, in so far as concerns said impeachment or trial. Refusal to comply with proper citation in this connection shall constitute contempt. [Obligatory.] (*Const., Art. viii, Sec. 2.*)

436. A Lodge cannot reconsider or rescind a vote granting a withdrawal card at the request of the brother holding the card. (*Jour. 1876, 1228, 1296.*)

437. Any Past Chancellor charged in a Grand Lodge, notice of which has been given to the Subordinate Lodge of which he is a member, ought not to be granted a withdrawal card; but if done so, either willfully or innocently, it can be annulled or recalled by action of the Lodge or *order* of the Grand Chancellor. (*Jour. 1873, App. 37.*)

The meaning evidently of the first line in this section is, that " Any Past Chancellor against whom charges had been brought in a Grand Lodge," etc.

438. If the card is procured by fraud, it is void; if through willfulness on the part of the Lodge, punish it; if issued innocently in absence of proper notice, etc., have it annulled. (*Jour. 1873, App. 37.*)

439. In any or all these cases the fact of holding the withdrawal card cannot be plead in bar of the proceedings, or the finding of same; and in *all* except the last would only add to the offenses for which already charged. (*Jour. 1873, App. 38.*)

(3) RENEWAL.

440. A withdrawal card can be renewed if lost or destroyed accidentally, and satisfactory evidence adduced from the holder and applicant, by the Lodge having granted the same, and upon such terms as the Lodge may determine. (*Const., Art. viii, Sec. 2.*)

441. Any brother who may have lost his withdrawal card can have the same renewed by applying to the source from which it emanated. (*Const., Art. viii, Sec. 2.*)

442. A Grand Lodge cannot compel a Lodge to renew an expired withdrawal card, when its by-laws provide that such renewal can only be obtained upon a ballot, two black balls rejecting the application. (*Jour. 1876, 1284, 1300.*)

443. Withdrawal cards are to be considered good until revoked or deposited, and all legislation inconsistent herewith is repealed. (*Jour. 1876, 1309.*)

This provision is doubtless to be construed prospectively; otherwise it would seem to conflict with the next preceding section. As the old decisions may, under this view, have some value as to cards issued immediately prior to this legislation, they are herewith presented :

Withdrawal cards, by the provisions on their face, cease to be of value twelve months from date. An applicant for affiliation by card, with an expired one, cannot be admitted or his proposition entertained until the card has been restored to vitality by a re-issue. See Art. VI [old] Subordinate Constitution: "A withdrawal card can be renewed after it has run out, by the Lodge having granted the same. and upon such terms as the Lodge may determine." The renewal of the card under that clause presumptively would be the payment of certain moneys. Such being the case, it seems that one year having elapsed, and the Lodge having been liberated from any claims of benefits that might have occurred, the reinstating the card or renewing its force would also reinstate a valid claim for the S. A. P. W. for term in which issued. (*Jour. 1873, App. 36.*)

A withdrawal card can be renewed after it has run out, by the Lodge which granted the same, and upon such terms as the Lodge may determine. (*Jour. 1872, 467, 468, 613.*)

It is proper, however, to state that a ruling has been made by the Supreme Chancellor, in a circular issued November 16. 1876, in which he rules: ",That *all* withdrawal cards not revoked or deposited are good, and may be received by any Lodge on deposit and application for membership." He states, however, that on this question the Committee on Laws and Supervision are not agreed.

(4) Rank Credentials.

444. All Knights having Past rank removing from one jurisdiction to another, and desiring to affiliate on a withdrawal card, must also present a rank credential to entitle him to the same. (*Const., Art. xxiv.*)

445. The rank of a brother to whom a withdrawal card is issued shall be stated on the card, and the form of the card shall be altered to conform to this legislation. (*Jour. 1876, 1309.*)

This legislation is a portion of a report of the Committee on Laws and Supervision (Jour. 1876, 1309), and was the action taken on certain recommendations made by the Supreme Chancellor (Jour. 1876. 1231), wherein he stated that " The law, as now understood, does not allow the rank of a member to appear on the withdrawal card. Much trouble has arisen on this account, as the Keepers of Records and Seals, attesting cards, often neglect to furnish a rank credential to accompany the card. I do not see the necessity of this law. and trust it may be abolished at this session. Hereafter direct that the rank of the member named in the card shall appear upon it."

Query, If the object of this legislation was to comply with these recommendations. upon which this is a report. then would not this be a contravention of the following clause of the present Constitution? " All Knights having Past rank removing from one jurisdiction to another, and desiring to affiliate on a withdrawal card, must also present a rank credential to entitle him to the same." If it was not with that view, then of what force or value is the insertion of the title on the card ?

Previous to this, withdrawal cards evidenced no rank in the Order of higher grade than that of Knight, and any prefix or affix thereto, setting forth that the bearer was a Past Chancellor or Past Grand Chancellor, was void, and of no value whatever as a credential of those two higher grades of rank. (*Jour. 1873, App. 35.*)

The following decisions were also made prior to the passage of this resolution, and are presented for the reasons given in the next preceding note:

The Past Official rank of Past Chancellor or Past Grand Chancellor must be evidenced by a certificate signed by the proper Grand Officers, duly attested with the Grand Lodge seal, prior to said Official rank being recognized when affiliating by card in any other Lodge than the one in which being a member where said rank was attained. (*Jour. 1873, App. 36.*)

A withdrawal card, with the prefix of "P. C." thereto, and the printed proceedings of the Grand Lodge of Ohio with a name the same as that appearing on the withdrawal card, as having been admitted and enrolled *as a* "P. C." in that Grand Lodge, are not sufficient evidence of the rank of P. C. The withdrawal card, although in regular form, carries no evidence of rank under the law higher than that of a Knight; and it cannot be claimed or admitted in any sense as a credential of rank or visiting card beyond the purposes as intended on its face. The printed proceedings are of weight so far as being unquestionably true, but in the absence of evidencing connection as between the claimant and the party therein set forth by an authenticated certificate are insufficient. (*Jour. 1873, App. 10.*)

On appeal of a Subordinate Lodge of the State of Kansas against the action of the Grand Lodge of that State in ordering said Subordinate Lodge to place P. C. on a withdrawal card of Kt. A., the law of the Grand Lodge Constitution reading as follows: "That a Past Chancellor, previous to being admitted as a member of the Grand Lodge, *must* present a certificate from his Lodge certifying that he had passed the chair of his Lodge;" it was resolved that the Grand Lodge of Kansas transcended the power of the Grand Lodge Constitution, and its action was reversed. (*Jour. 1876, 1306.*)

(5) CARRY S. A. P. W. FOR HOW LONG.

446. The refusal of the Supreme Lodge to adopt a form of withdrawal card expressing on its face "the bearer of it shall be entitled to the S. A. P. W. for *one year*" (Jour. 1872, 536–7, 579), firmly establishes the principle that it only carries the S. A. P. W. for the term *in which issued.* There being no specific legislation or decision on the point of a renewed issue by the proper Grand Officers in case of a suspended or defunct Lodge, it *does* carry the S. A. P. W. with it *for the term in which issued*, but *no longer.* (*Jour. 1873, App. 36.*)

(6) CANNOT BE USED AS VISITING CARDS.

447. Withdrawal cards cannot and must *not* be used for or recognized in *any* sense as "visiting cards." The

Supreme obligatory law is *imperative* on the point that "no visiting cards shall be used in the Order." (*Jour. 1868, 18.*) Therefore, when presented in that sense, they *must* be refused. If having the S. A. P. W., they are not required to be shown by the visitor. If not having the S. A. P. W., they are valueless to get it, *unless* accompanied by an order from the Lodge by which issued, signed by the Chancellor Commander, attested by the seal and signature of the K. R. and S., *and then* ONLY *for the term in which the card was issued.* (*Jour. 1873, App. 36.*)

[See, also, note to Sec. 445, *ante.*]

(7) In Cases of Defunct Lodges.

448. In jurisdictions where no Grand Lodge exists, and the books of a defunct Lodge cannot be had to ascertain the standing of an applicant for a withdrawal card, the practice, as stated by the Supreme Chancellor, has been first to become satisfied that the applicant was formerly a member of the defunct Lodge, and then issue the card upon payment of $2. (*Jour. 1876, 1231.*)

449. A person who has received the initiatory rank of Page in a Lodge of one jurisdiction, which, before he has an opportunity to receive the other ranks, becomes defunct, and who, after a lapse of time, applies to a Lodge in another State for the other ranks, would be entitled to a card issued from the Grand Lodge under the jurisdiction of which he was a member, which he would be entitled to deposit in another jurisdiction as in other cases. (*Jour. 1876, 1311, 1314.*)

Though the case on which this is a decision was where the application for advancement was made in *another jurisdiction*, yet, by parity of reasoning, and in view of the absence of any more direct legislation, this would seem justly to apply to a case where the party desired advancement in the same jurisdiction where the Lodge originally existed.

(8) Effect of Issue in Irregular Form.

450. On appeal of W. from the action of the Grand Lodge of New Jersey, in 1876, the facts were as follows: W., the appellant, was a member of Good Samaritan Lodge, No. 52, in good and regular standing, until June, 1871, when he moved to Trenton, New Jersey. In August following he asked for a withdrawal card, which was granted, as appears by the minutes of Good Samaritan Lodge. The Lodge, at the time, had no printed withdrawal cards, and application was made to the Grand Keeper of Records and Seal, who answered that he had none at the time, but promised to furnish them in a short time. Good Samaritan Lodge, in place of a withdrawal card, sent, under seal, a certificate, which certificate was accepted by the Grand Chancellor of New Jersey as sufficient evidence of the good standing of W.; whereupon Pythias Lodge, No. 61, was instituted, and W. made Worthy Chancellor and installed as such. Since the Lodge was instituted W. was made trustee of the Lodge; was elected and served as representative of Pythias Lodge in the Grand Lodge of New Jersey. In 1874 a question was raised in Pythias Lodge as to the good standing of W., it being urged that he was not then, and, indeed, had not been, a member of Pythias Lodge, No. 61, which position was sustained by the Grand Lodge of New Jersey. Upon the appeal to the Supreme Lodge, it was, in view of the facts in the case — that W.'s not having a card in regular form was no fault of his; that, from testimony, he originated Pythias Lodge, and acted with it, bearing his portion of all its burdens until quite recently; that no charges had been preferred against him; that all concerned were, at the time, and have ever since been, acting in good faith: *Resolved*, that W. was a Past Chancellor in good standing and a member of Pythias Lodge, No. 61. (*Jour. 1876, 1305, 1306.*)

While this would establish the general principle that a Lodge has no right to take advantage of its own error to the detriment of an innocent party, yet it should not be accepted as in any way countenancing, directly or indirectly, the right on the part of a Lodge to the issuance of any other than the prescribed card. If they have none on hand, that is their own fault — they should always be provided with them.

WRITS OF ERROR.
[See Appeals.]

WRITTEN AND UNWRITTEN WORK.
[See Supreme Lodge ; Constitutions.]

451. The Written and Unwritten Work, which cannot be altered, except as provided in Art. XXXIII of Supreme Lodge Constitution, consists :

1. Of the Work and its explanations, as contained and illustrated in the Book of Diagrams in the hands of the Supreme Chancellor.

2. Of the lectures, charges, obligations and all written work contained in the Ritual, and included in the forms and ceremonies for opening and closing the Lodge, passing from rank to rank and conferring the different grades of rank.

3. The forms and ceremonies as prescribed for installation and funeral.

4. The forms and ceremonies as prescribed for opening and closing a Grand Lodge, and installing the officers thereof, as contained in the Grand Lodge Ritual, and also for conferring Past Chancellor's rank as contained in the same.

5. The forms and ceremonies as laid down in Supreme Lodge Ritual.

(*Jour. 1876, 1293.*)

This is the report of the Committee on Laws and Supervision, in answer to a question by Rep. Cotter, of Kentucky (Jour. 1876, 1282), wherein he desired that the Written and Unwritten Work should be designated, and the committee seem to have omitted to include the "Dedication Ceremonies."

INDEX.